WAGES
OF
SIN

WAGES
OF
SIN

Angela Jarvis

ABSOLUTELY AMA⚡ING eBOOKS

ABSOLUTELY AMAZING eBOOKS

Published by Whiz Bang LLC, 926 Truman Avenue, Key West, Florida 33040, USA.

For information contact:
Publisher@AbsolutelyAmazingEbooks.com

ISBN-13: 978-1945772641 (Absolutely Amazing Ebooks)

ISBN-10: 1945772646

Although there have been a lot of people who have been part of my journey, I dedicate my first book to my one true love and soul mate, my husband Kevin. You have always stood by me, always having the blind faith in me that I could do anything I set my mind to. Not once have you ever thought my dreams were out of reach and have always encouraged me to pursue them.

Te Amo Mucho.

WAGES
OF
SIN

PROLOGUE

He was in a hurry.

Any minute now the man who rode his bike this way every morning was bound to show up. He had not been thinking clearly or he would not have chosen this time of day to bring the girl out here. Sometimes his mind would get that foggy feeling followed soon after by a headache, and the decisions he made during that time were not always the best.

The girl was small in height and very light weight, so carrying her wasn't too big a burden, but he still broke a sweat in the early morning Florida heat. The sun was not up yet, but it was already reaching the point of stifling.

The sweat stung his eyes as he bent over to lay her down among the thatch palms. He reached up to wipe the sweat away with his forearm, but that didn't work, because it too was covered in dampness. He wore rubber gloves so as not to leave behind fingerprints on anything he might touch, and that was causing his hands to sweat profusely, but it was necessary. He lived life off the radar and planned on keeping it that way.

He squeezed his eyes shut for a moment hoping to keep the sweat from running down into his eyes, but it only caused them to burn, as the sweat managed to get in anyway. He opened his eyes to resume his task.

He had chosen her final resting place to be where he had spotted her a little over a month ago. He watched her on and off for several days as she took her daily jogs. She always ended up taking a break here at this nature refuge just off the side of the road. He had first seen her at the shelter in Key West for women. Thinking she might be a resident there, he watched her and soon realized she volunteered there. It wasn't until he saw her again that he recognized her running down Key Deer Boulevard in navy blue jogging pants and a tight white T-shirt.

The T-shirt did little to conceal her more than ample breasts bouncing up and down. The only way a woman could jog with breasts that large was if they were implants. That led him to his next question.

What did she do for a living?

By following her, he learned that she worked in a waterfront restaurant that delighted male customers by the servers dressing in next to nothing uniforms. He continued to watch for a while to see what her daily routines were like. Often, she would go down the little trail that led to Blue Hole observation deck. There she would sit and catch her breath, drink a few sips of water, stretch a little and then return the way she came. He had visited the small observation deck that overlooked the pond and observed every angle to see where her final resting place would be. He finally chose this spot. It could not be seen, not very clearly anyway, from the deck and was not easily accessible from the nature trail that all the tourists took around the small pond ... any decomposition smell would be attributed to the death of one of many animals that were plentiful on the island, and were often times struck by cars.

He took his foot and tried to cover her up with pine needles and leaves, but this time of year was just not the season that lends itself to leaves being plentiful. He took out the pocket knife his grandfather had given him as a child, and cut some fronds off a thatch palm and used them to cover the girl's body.

He looked at her face one last time, and placed the last frond over her head. He almost felt a twinge of what could have been called pity.

Almost.

He did not really know what pity felt like, or any other emotion for that matter. Love, hate, guilt, anger, happiness, were just words to him. Trying to describe those emotions to him would be like describing colors to a blind person.

He learned how to emulate these emotions and eventually convinced everyone he was "normal." Sadly, there were things he would never forget and one of those things was the punishment he had to endure as a child; or all he had felt then was physical pain.

Pain he knew, and knew well.

He stepped around her body careful not to disturb her resting place. Now, all that was left to do was get out of here before anyone saw him. On an island the size of Big Pine Key, with a population of around 5000 people, it sounded a lot easier than it was. Walking through the brush he came to the edge of the wooded area, and cautiously peered through the trees. He saw no one, so he stepped out of the cool dampness of the woods and into the sun that was just beginning to light the morning sky. Cautiously, he made his way back to his car, cranking it and relishing the cool air blowing in his face.

So far so good.

He knew this was his true calling in life. His other "job" was one that he had chosen to convince society that he was just like everyone else, and he had fooled them all.

He chuckled to himself. If they only knew. Now, to seek out the next lost girl who needed his *help*.

CHAPTER 1

Al Foster hummed the tune to his favorite song "I'm Living on Key West Time" by one of his favorite singers and friend Howard Livingston, as he biked down Key Deer Boulevard. He was wearing his official retirement uniform consisting of a tie-dyed T-shirt and bandana that matched the tie-dyed painted three-wheeled bike he rode, which in itself was an attraction on Big Pine Key.

Often times, the tourists that vacationed here would snap his picture as he pedaled by waving, and sometimes he would stop and pose with them. It seemed he rarely met a stranger, and if it was someone he had never met, they weren't strangers for long. He was very friendly by nature, and welcomed everyone to this little island paradise he called home. He had even managed to convince a few people to buy homes here and become residents themselves. He thought about being a real estate broker if he ever found himself needing to work again, but he sure as hell hoped that would never be the case. His retirement income was modest, but allowed him to realize his dream of living in the Florida Keys.

Although Big Pine Key has roughly 5800 acres and is big in comparison to Key West, it doesn't have as many residents. One of the biggest draws for tourists to the island is the fact that it is home to the famous Key Deer. The miniature version of white-tailed deer is considered an endangered species. Living in such close proximity to humans, they have grown accustomed to people and have little fear. They love eating hibiscus flowers and other plants along the roadsides and often wander into people's yards to nibble on their plants. The residents don't mind because they are so beautiful and small, and are often thought of as neighborhood pets, although that is highly discouraged by the local authorities.

Al came here quite a bit when he was a younger man and decided long ago that this would be where he would live when he retired from teaching high school. Life could not be much sweeter, and he counted his lucky stars every day that things had worked out the way they had.

There had been a rough series of events, including a painful divorce, that led him here, but this is where he belonged, and this is where he would stay until the day he took his final breath.

He finally arrived at the Blue Hole and parked his bike near the rack in the parking lot that accommodated five cars at best. There was no need to lock his bike because no one here would bother it. People here were different than most places. He never locked the door on his house, not even at night when going to bed.

He grabbed his camera out of the basket of the bike, and was eager to walk down to the wooden deck that served as an overlook to observe the natural foliage and wildlife that lived in the area. There were trails that one could take into the wooded areas around the water and there was always an abundance of small animals and birds to snap pictures of. It was a pleasant retreat from the harsh Florida heat that somehow always managed to feel cooler down the trails. Right before he got to the observation deck, he took a small path to the right. It was here about a month ago, where he found a Heron's nest with two baby blue eggs in it, and he was eagerly awaiting the hatching of the baby birds. He was hoping to get pictures of them when they were newly hatched, so he had been coming here diligently every day for the past few weeks. He spotted the mama Heron by the feathers on her head and back that were so black they had a blue hue when the sunlight hit them at just the right angle. He gave as much effort to being quiet as he could but he stepped on a twig and as it snapped, she startled and flew off toward the Blue Hole. Damn! He would try again later. He did manage to see the two eggs in the nest and got a couple shots of them before backing away and going around the corner to the observation deck.

Smiling to himself, he took in the natural beauty of this serene place in the morning stillness. He walked to the railing and looked over the edge, and like clockwork, the gator that lived there saw him and came gliding over.

"I see ya!" Al said as he grinned and lifted his camera. "Smile and show me those pearly whites!" He took a couple of snapshots of the alligator and out of the corner of his eye spotted the heron that had taken off from the nest a few minutes earlier. It was circling the sky around the water trying to determine if it was safe to return to the nest. He aimed his camera focusing in to capture her winging her way back home. She swooped low in the sky and was flying about fifteen feet above the water. He fired rapid shots to get her in flight. About the fourth picture in, he caught the glare of something shiny in the background. He continued on until the heron was safely back into the trees where her nest was tucked away.

Curious, he peered through the lens towards the approximate spot he had seen the reflection. He focused his lens to allow the strongest zoom magnification and moved the camera slowly from left to right, trying to catch a glimpse of what he saw earlier. Maybe it was just the glare of sunlight reflecting off the water, he thought. He saw it again. Looking through the lens he just could not tell what he was looking at.

Deciding to check it out on his way back, he made his way around to the heron's nest once more before leaving. The new mom was sitting prim and proper on her eggs and this time he managed to get the shot he was trying for.

Hanging the camera around his neck, he walked back down the path to the parking lot. Thinking that the reflection he saw might be broken glass, he grabbed a black plastic garbage bag out of the basket on his bike. Broken glass could actually cause the grass to catch fire so he tried to pick it up whenever he saw it.

He made his way down a slightly overgrown trail off the right side of the parking area that led to a wooded area on the opposite side of the water from the observation deck. He could see the deck from here and stopped to take a couple of pictures from this vantage point, one he had never seen before, but unique in its own beauty.

He looked around on the ground for glass fragments, but couldn't find any. He walked a little bit further in observing the air plants blooming on the side of the taller pines. They were stunning at this time of the year. He aimed his camera and was stepping backward to get a better angle when he almost tripped. Looking down he expected to see a fallen log. What he saw shook him to his core.

"Oh God ... Oh My God!" It was a human leg. He was too scared to move another inch. Soon his good sense overrode his shock and he backed away slowly. When he reached the halfway point of the trail, he turned and ran fumbling around in his pocket for his cell phone. Immediately he dialed 911 trying to control the shaking in his hands.

"911, what's your emergency?"

"I'd like to report a body in the woods by Blue Hole."

~ ~ ~

Finally, after what seemed like a lifetime, Al could hear the wailing of sirens in the distance growing closer. He let out a sigh of relief. Soon, he was surrounded by deputies and an ambulance. A lot of good an ambulance was going to do for that poor soul, he thought.

He walked towards the car with officers stepping out and directed them towards the wooded area where the body was. He was asked not to leave, so he crossed his arms and leaned against the hood of one of the patrol cars. Two officers disappeared down the path into the woods.

A few minutes later, a burly detective walked over to him. Poor guy, Al thought. His necktie was so tight it gave the impression it was pinching off the blood flow to his head causing his face to flush bright red. In reality, it was probably just the heat.

"Detective Morris" he said sticking out his hand in a very matter of fact greeting.

"Al Foster" he replied, shaking the detective's hand.

"Mr. Foster, I would like you to give a statement to Officer Phillips about what exactly happened leading up to you finding the body. Be sure to leave your phone number and address with him."

The detective waved the officer over and gave him instructions to take Al's statement. He left walking towards his patrol car and dialing his cell phone. The detective needed an expert on this case and was calling the station to see if they had reached her yet.

Al followed Officer Phillips to the car where he handed him a clipboard and was given instructions on how to fill out the report. Attached was a form with several questions and a blank area to describe what he had witnessed. Using the hood of the car for a temporary desk, it took him about 15 minutes to fill it out .He signed the bottom of the form declaring that the above statement was the truth and as accurate as his memory could recall. He returned the clipboard to the officer, who didn't look old enough to have too many years on the force.

"Sir, you need to stay here awhile longer until Detective Morris says you are free to go."

"Ok, but do you mind if I sit on my bike?" Al asked.

"No sir, that would be fine."

Al walked over to his bike and sat down. He didn't realize how shaky he felt until that very moment. It must be the adrenaline rush finally slowing down. He removed the camera from around his neck, and felt relief from the weight of it. What a morning! He would love to go home and have a beer to steady his nerves, not to mention to quench his thirst in this heat, but it looked like that wasn't happening anytime soon.

Al looked around and noticed quite a few joggers and bicyclists had started gathering around curious as to what the sheriff's department was doing. He wondered how much longer he was going to be here so, out of boredom, he picked up his camera and started taking pictures of the people in the crowd. He was by no means a detective of any sort, and the only knowledge he had about police work came from cop and crime dramas on TV, but he wondered if the person responsible was in the crowd. He had heard that the criminals often return to the scene of the crime.

It took a moment for that thought to sink in.

The scene of a crime right here on peaceful Big Pine Key, where crime rarely took place except for the occasional shoplifter at the local Winn Dixie.

He wondered how this would affect life in his little slice of paradise. He sat there watching the different cops and the coroner's office employees going in and out of the woods. He snapped a couple of pictures of them too. Eventually, they began to leave and a small dark-haired lady started towards him. She had a badge clipped to the waistband of her jeans. Maybe she was coming to tell him he could leave. Then, he was going to go home and drink the biggest beer he could find.

Chapter 2

Arriving at the crime scene was a nightmare. There was nowhere to park so Detective Valerie Mason had to cautiously finagle her way around a crowd of curious onlookers to try to find a spot without running someone over. Thankfully, a Fish and Game Wildlife officer cleared a spot and she pulled the Explorer off on the side of the road. Knowing what she would face when she opened the door, she quickly pulled her shoulder length black tresses back and up into a ponytail. She kept a package of elastic bands in her truck console for just such occasions, which was more often than not these days as she stepped from the coolness of the air-conditioned patrol truck. It was too damn hot to be 9:30 in the morning. The humidity of the Florida Keys was as thick as pea soup. Sweat popped out on her forehead and the bridge of her nose.

"How is it even possible to sweat as soon as you step into the heat?" she asked herself as she reached up to wipe the dampness away with the backside of her palm.

She saw a small crowd gathered at the edge of a wooded area next to the Blue Hole parking lot, if you wanted to call it that. It was more like a place to pull off. She noticed the white coroners van was here, which meant her best friend and colleague Delaney Summers was probably on the scene as well. She had just been named acting Medical Examiner to replace the one that had retired suddenly, and without explanation. It gave her the distinction of being the youngest ME in the county at the age of thirty-two.

Yellow police tape had already been put up to keep the onlookers back, and as she approached it, an aging, partially bald detective, motioned for her to come towards him. She walked past the residents and tourists to duck under the tape as he held it up as far it would stretch for her to pass underneath it.

"Detective David Morris." he said, sticking his meaty hand out in introduction.

"Hi, Detective Valerie Mason" she replied, gripping his hand to shake it and instantly regretting it. It was slick with sweat and that really grossed her out. She had an urge to wipe it on her pants, but quickly quelled it so as not to offend him.

"I have heard all about you Detective Mason!" he said with a genuine smile. "We know you are good at what you do, so that is why we want you in on this. We normally don't have crimes of this nature out here on Big Pine Key. Word has it you've handled quite a bit of this stuff in Broward County before you moved down here, so we knew you were the woman for the job."

"Well I am flattered Detective Morris, but what exactly is *it* that we have here?" she asked, to keep him from doling out more compliments. Not that she didn't appreciate it, but not being used to such praise, it was a little embarrassing.

"It's a damn shame is what it is!" he spat out with a soft southern drawl. "A young woman, looks to be in her early twenties. Just lying there as if she were sleeping. She was found by that fella over there, who looks like a throwback from the sixties. He just finished filling out his statement. Mighty suspicious to me that he just happened to be out here picking up trash and saw her back there. Who picks up trash voluntarily, especially in this heat?"

Valerie turned to look at the man that Detective Morris has pointed out. He was sitting on his three-wheeled bike. He did look like a throwback from the sixties, a flower child or hippie, whatever they were called, with a tie-dyed shirt and bandana around hair that was white as snow. The bike was unlike anything she had ever seen before, and she had seen a lot of different things and types of people in the Keys.

Down here, anything goes.

"Let's go take a look and see if we can figure out a few things." She followed the burly detective down a small winding path and was so thankful for the coolness that the tall pines provided. It had to be at least ten degrees cooler in here than out in the hot open sun.

"When we got to the body, it was covered up with fronds from thatch palms. I guess the killer was trying to hide the body. You can see where they've been cut with a knife or some other type of blade." The detective explained to her as they walked down the narrow dirt path that she would hardly call a nature trail. Moss and vines hung down out of trees and she had to constantly push them out of her face, some of them wanting to stick to her skin because of the sweat.

Great, she thought, I hope none of these are poison ivy! Thick underbrush on either side of the path was sure to be full of little critters and snakes. She could not handle snakes, but she had a job to do.

The path led around to the backside of the Blue Hole which could only be seen after stepping around some underbrush and into a small clearing. From here the observation deck that many tourists stood on to take pictures of the alligator that made his home there could be seen, but not very well, so she wondered if you could see this spot from the observation deck. If so, there might have been witnesses. Making a mental note to go around and check that out, she turned back to where a small form lay on the ground, while her friend was examining the body. She turned to a crime scene tech and asked for a pair of gloves, and after sliding them on she knelt down as Delaney looked up from the body.

"Hey Val."

"Hey yourself. Anything you can tell us?"

"Young girl between the ages of eighteen and twenty-five. There are bruises around her throat indicating strangulation, but that doesn't necessarily mean that is the COD. The pine needles around the left side of the body have been disturbed. It could be from her struggling against whoever did this as she was dying. My bet is that they are from the person that put her out here, but that's for you guys to figure out. I think you are looking at a secondary crime scene. Her liver temp tells me she has been dead for about twelve hours now, that and the fact she is in full rigor. These woods have animals that would have been here by now for a meal if she had been here all that time. I see no outward signs of sexual assault. All of her clothes are on including her shoes. Most of the time after a rape, the rapist doesn't bother to redress the victim. I'll be able to tell for sure though once I get her back to the lab."

Valerie could see that Detective Morris had been correct in his description of the victim. It looked as if she had fallen asleep, except for the bruises around her throat. Her hair was bleached blonde with black streaks going through it. Typical for younger girls to have two very drastic hair colors wanting to make a statement.

Her own sister had neon pink tips last summer. She wondered if they had grown out by now.

Shaking her head to clear her mind, she needed to focus on the task at hand and not her sister. The victim was wearing jogging pants, and a T-shirt with nice running shoes. There was a small gold bracelet around her right wrist. It looked as if it once had something engraved on it, perhaps her name, but now it was worn down with time. They would need to examine it closely. It reminded her of the bracelets she and her sister had been given from their mother on their last Christmas together.

No matter how many times she saw this kind of thing, it still got to her. Each time there was a small fear that it might be her sister when she looked into the face of a victim. Clearing her mind of those personal and unpleasant thoughts once again, she continued her brief evaluation of the body. She looked around to see if there were footprints, but there were too much natural debris for anyone to leave any. So, did she walk in here and get attacked, or had the crime taken place elsewhere making this a secondary crime scene, like Delaney had suggested? She sighed inwardly at the atrocities that people inflicted upon one another and started to stand.

"I guess we can move her now, there's nothing else we can do from here. The crime-scene techs have already taken their photographs. The evidence on her body needed to be preserved for the autopsy. It looks like the rain might come in a little early today so we need to get the poor thing out of here," Delaney said, as she observed rain clouds building in the southern sky. They were still pretty far off, but this was Florida, and as the old saying goes *if you don't like the weather here, just wait 5 minutes.*

"Saunders," Morris barked at a young officer who didn't look old enough to carry a gun, much less be an officer of the law. He had been standing back observing everything and looking as if he had seen a ghost.

"Yes sir?" hoping he wouldn't be required to do anything that included touching the body. Until now he had done nothing but arrest a shoplifter every now and again and write tickets to speeders going through Big Pine at night where the speed limit was posted thirty five mph due to the Key Deer being more active after sundown. This was the first actual dead body he had ever seen in person. He had seen plenty in Police Academy videos, but it was not even close to the real thing. It did help that she looked so peaceful and there was no blood anywhere, but still it was a dead body!

"Go see if the coroner needs help loading the victim into the back of the van and then meet me back at the station." He shook his head at the young man as he walked away. It was as if he had read the poor kids thoughts. Seeing how uncomfortable the young man looked, Delaney stated they needed no help. She hated the way more experienced officers seem to enjoy picking on the young and inexperienced. She went through plenty of it herself. Before she became a medical examiner, she had wanted to be a cop. After some of the stuff she had seen her rookie year, she decided she would much rather deal with the dead than the living. She could help the dead by figuring out what happened in their last moments, but the living, she was pretty sure there was no hope for.

"Are you coming by the station Detective Mason?" Morris said.

"I will meet you there later, but first I want to look around and get a feel for the area. I know your crime scene techs know what they're doing, but I still would like to do a little investigating on my own. I also want to talk to the man that found the girl."

He looked at her thoughtfully for a few seconds and said, "I noticed you keep referring to the victim as "the girl" instead of the victim. Why is that?"

"Detective Morris, although she is technically our victim, she is definitely someone's daughter and possibly someone's sister." she said with a little catch in her voice, more so than she had intended. He looked a little surprised.

"Sorry. I just never heard anyone refer to a victim like that...." He trailed off.

She blew out her breath and realized she had probably sounded unprofessional.

"No, I'm sorry, I guess this heat is getting to me and making me a little cranky. Please accept my apology." She certainly didn't want to get off on the wrong foot with any of the officers here.

"I know exactly what you mean about the heat. Don't worry about it, no harm done. I'll see you back at the station when you're through here." He walked away leaving her to do her own investigating. She would start with the witness, and then she would make a trip to the other side of Blue Hole to the observation deck to see if it was possible someone could have seen or heard something. The problem was if someone did see something, would they come forward with the information? A lot of times witnesses were afraid to get involved.

She started tracking her way back to the entrance of the trail when about halfway down, a sliver of paper caught her eye. It was so small and about fifteen feet off the side of the trail that it would have probably gone unnoticed by the crime scene techs, or they thought it was inconsequential. She reached over and picked it up. It was no larger than a couple of square inches and the edges were frayed. It was damp from the morning dew, and maybe from the afternoon rains that were becoming more frequent with this time of year. No wording was legible and all she could make out was what looked like the letter T with an S wrapped around it. Nothing important, she thought, but she stuffed it in her pocket. She would throw it in the trash later. She hated litter.

She went in search of the man who stumbled upon the scene this morning. Stepping out of the coolness of the wooded area and back into the heat was enough to take her breath away. Damn, could it get any hotter? She should really be careful what she asked for even if it was sarcastically, she supposed. She scanned the now dwindling crowd for the old hippie on the unique tie-dyed painted bike and found him sitting under the shade of a pine tree messing with a camera, right where she had seen him last before following Detective Morris into the woods.

She quickly walked over to him thinking he had waited long enough in this heat and introduced herself.

"You must be Detective Mason." He said very matter-of-fact.

"Yes, I am, and your name?"

"Al Foster. Pleased to meet you. Other circumstances would have been nicer though."

"Yes sir, can't argue with that. That is a very interesting paint job you have there on your bike," she said, smiling in spite of the situation.

"Thank you! Tie-dyed is my favorite color." he replied with a small grin causing her to smile once again. What an odd fellow, but surprisingly, she felt at ease in his presence.

"Well, down to business Mr. Foster. Can you tell me how you happened to find this young woman?"

"Certainly. I ride my bike along this road every morning. Sometimes I jog, but this morning was way too hot for that. I stop to take pictures along the way if I see something interesting, photography has always been a hobby of mine. I also bring a garbage bag to pick up trash along the roadside because I volunteer for the Key Deer Refuge, so I help out by picking it up as I see it." He pointed to a couple of black plastic trash bags in the basket of his bike alongside his camera.

"When I got to Blue Hole this morning I parked my bike and went to take pictures of a Heron's nest that has eggs in it. I am hoping to capture the newborn chicks when they hatch. Afterwards, I went to the observation deck and saw the alligator that lives there was out sunning so I took a few shots of him. The heron that had been in her nest earlier was flying around and I turned my camera to get a shot of her in flight. I noticed a shiny reflection through my lens coming from the other side of the water. I focused in as best I could to see if I could figure out what it was but couldn't find it again. My first thought was that it was broken glass from the beer bottles that the kids leave behind sometimes, and in this heat, a piece of glass could start a fire. So, when I left there, I took a garbage bag and went in that direction from the bike rack to see about picking up the glass. Turned out to be something far worse than beer bottles. I didn't waste any time calling 911."

"Did you see anyone out here this morning?"

"I didn't, but to be honest even if I had, I wouldn't have thought anything about it. People come and go out here all the time."

"Do people go back there a lot too?" she asked pointing to the trail that led to the crime scene.

"Not really. There is a path that leads around the left side of the Hole that all the tourists use but this far back, if and when it is used, it's usually teenagers drinking or looking for a place to make out."

"Can I get your phone number and home address in case I have more questions?

"Sure." He waited for a moment for her to take out a small notebook or piece of paper to write on but when she didn't he finished, "I gave it to the officer but my number is 555-2782,

It's a cell. I don't have a home phone. My address is 227 Hibiscus Lane. It's about 1 ½ miles up the road from here."

"Ok. Well thank you for your help, and for sticking around in this heat Mr. Foster. I'll be in touch."

She started to walk away but he stopped her by asking, "I'm curious. You didn't write anything down that I've told you. How are you going to remember everything I said?"

"You gave your written statement to an officer earlier so if there is any reason why I can't remember, I'll refer to his report. 555-2782, right? And 227 Hibiscus Lane?" She just had a knack for remembering numbers.

"Impressive!"

"It can be nice and other times a pain. It crowds the mind sometimes with unwanted junk, but comes in handy on the job."

"All in the way you look at life. The glass half empty, half full thing you know," he said smiling again. "Never let a gift go to waste."

"I'm sure we'll be talking again."

"I don't know if it will help or anything, but as I was waiting to be released, I took pictures of the crowd and everything that was going on earlier if you need to take a look."

"Thanks. I'll let you know if I need them."

What an odd man. Not in a bad way, just different, and she could tell by his eyes that he had a very kind soul. She found herself really hoping he had nothing to do with this, although her intuition told her he didn't.

As she made her way back to her truck she heard him humming a tune that sounded familiar to her, and turned and watched as he headed back down the road in the direction he said he lived. He stopped soon after and she saw him take a picture of an Osprey nested on top of a utility pole. He must have sensed her watching him because he turned to her and waved. She raised her hand slightly and waved back as she opened the back window of the Explorer to load the bag of trash in the back. She was just about to get in and turn on the ignition so she could crank the air condition up when she remembered she had to visit the observation deck to see if she could get a clear view of the crime scene from the deck.

"Damn!" she said as she climbed back out into the stifling heat, and started down the little path that would lead her to the deck.

Chapter 3

Val entered one of the smallest sheriff substations she had ever been in. It had once been an office space for a cell phone company until 3 years ago, when it was transformed into a substation when the phone company went bankrupt. She was greeted by the coolness of air conditioning and the strong smell of coffee that had been kept hot for several hours too long. Still, it made her mouth water. Her aunt once told her that coffee was one of life's biggest disappointments, because it never tasted as good as it smelled. Val certainly did not agree with that observation most of the time, but her aunt was probably on the money with that particular pot over in the corner. She only had a half cup this morning when she had received the call to come out to Big Pike Key, but decided against making a cup now, because it was almost noon and it was much too hot outside for it. Besides that, she had a hard enough time sleeping at night without adding any more caffeine. The sound of voices murmuring could be heard around the station floor and she noticed deputies talking to several people she was certain were residents, trying to reassure them. The phone seemed to be ringing nonstop and there were several people answering calls that they probably did not consider part of their normal job description.

She looked around for Detective Morris, not seeing him anywhere. She walked over to a desk where a petite blonde sat trying to juggle the phone calls coming in about the murder, judging from the part of the conversation she could hear. Word must have spread around the little island pretty fast. She looked up with a smile and held up a finger indicating for Val to wait a minute.

"Ma'am, we don't have many details right now, but I'm sure you have nothing to worry about. If you see something suspicious, call us ok." She finally hung up with a huge sigh.

"Rough morning huh?" Val said grinning.

"The phone has been ringing off the hook! I can't believe how fast word got around already!"

"Well, it is a small island with a lot of retired people who have nothing but time on their hands to gossip!" Val said. "Can you tell me where to find Detective Morris?"

"He was back in his office a few minutes ago. Go down the hallway, it's the second door on the right."

"Thanks." Valerie replied then headed down the hall. She approached the second door and saw it was half open but knocked out of courtesy anyway.

"Come on in," Detective Morris said looking up and then seeing who it was, he acknowledged her with a smile. "Detective Mason, have a seat."

"Thank you sir," She smiled back. His enthusiasm seemed to be contagious.

"Did you find anything else after I left the scene?"

"No sir, I didn't. I went out to the observation deck but the crime scene wasn't clearly visible from there. Unless someone was using the same path that the girl was found on, I don't think we are going to have any witnesses other than the one who found her."

"What do you think about him? Think he could be our guy?"

"Every instinct tells me no. I think he just happened to find her just like he said."

"Well, we have our work cut out for us then, but for now he is all we have. From what I could see at the crime scene, the killer did not leave us much to go on. We did get the bag that the witness had been putting trash in. I'll give it over to CSI as soon as possible."

"Maybe the autopsy will give us more definitive answers, hopefully some DNA that we could use."

"It's only good if he is already in the system, as you know, but we can keep our fingers crossed."

"I plan on making a call to the coroner as soon as I get back to Key West. I'll ask her to call me as soon as she has anything so I can pick a report. I can fax it to you, or if I happen to be in the area, I'll bring it to you myself."

"I appreciate it. Not to change the subject, but have you had lunch yet? I am starving." A quick glance at the man's stomach and one could tell he was definitely *not* starving.

"I was going to head back, but come to think of it, I could eat."

"I know just the place. Let me tell Missy where we will be in case she needs something and then we will get some of the best pizza you have ever had! "

"The best pizza? In the Keys? You're kidding, right?"

"Just you wait! You'll see!" he said wagging his finger at her and smiling.

They walked back down the hall to the front desk where she had spoken to the young lady earlier when coming in. The detective told her they would be having lunch out on No Name Key at one of the best-hidden secrets of the islands. If she needed anything just give him a call on his cell.

"OOOH, can you bring me some pizza back please?" Missy asked almost begging.

"Sure can," he said grinning and giving Val the I-told-you-so look. They walked out together and he told her to follow him so she wouldn't have to come back to the station to get her Explorer when they were finished ... His directions included just around the corner and down the road a piece. She was glad he didn't program GPS's for a living. Once on the road, she had to laugh, because he wasn't kidding. They went around the corner and then down the road a few miles, just a little ways to North Watson Boulevard and there it was. They pulled up to a small building that wasn't fancy looking, and didn't have much room for parking. What was it with these islands and no parking spaces?

Once she finally maneuvered her Explorer in behind his on the side of the road, they got out and walked up to the door. The smell of food coming from inside was amazing. It made her mouth water and then she realized how thirsty she was also. She normally kept some bottled water in a small cooler in her truck. You could certainly suffer dehydration and heat stroke easily down here in the heat, but she had no time this morning for that.

Upon entering the restaurant, she was intrigued. The place was not large, but bigger than it looked from outside. It was dark on the interior but gave the feeling of a cool retreat from the heat. One-dollar bills hung from the ceiling and covered the walls like wallpaper. When a draft of the air conditioning touched them they would softly flap around like wind chimes only making a whisper of sound. Someone could make a small fortune should they ever decide to rob this place. It was certainly a unique way to decorate. The waitress approached and acknowledged them.

"Hey there David. How ya' doing?"

"Fine Mary Anne. Yourself?"

"Just peachy darling. What can I get you folks to drink?"

"I'll have a sweet tea and ... where are my manners? This is Detective Valerie Mason," he said nodding towards Val. "She is out here helping us work on a case."

"Nice to meet you Detective." She said extending her hand out for a polite shake.

"You can call me Val. There's no need to be formal, and I will have unsweet tea if you have it."

"We do. You out here helping on the murder of that poor young girl? I heard about it after I got to work this morning."

"I am."

"Well let me get your drink order in for ya'll. I'll be right back."

"Unsweet tea? Girl, were you born in the south?" Detective Morris teased.

"Actually it is pretty bad because I was born in a little town named Clewiston on the south end of Lake Okeechobee. You know America's Sweetest Town? Named that for the massive amounts of sugar cane fields and the industry that has kept it alive and well for he past one hundred years or so. Some might call me a traitor!" she answered with a huge grin.

Shaking his head he replied, "Guess you'll never be asked to be their spokesperson, huh?"

"Not very likely."

Mary Anne returned with the glasses of tea and asked if they were ready to order. Val waited on Detective Morris to order one of those pizzas this place was supposed to be famous for, and he did just that. Once Mary Anne walked away from the table he asked, "Well, getting back to business, do you think this was an isolated incident?"

"I sure hope so. It could have been a domestic situation, but that doesn't fit because of the lack of evidence at the scene. Whoever it was seemed to know what they were doing."

"I was thinking the same thing. I'll have some patrols in that area to see if anyone comes around that looks suspicious. Let's see if they return to the scene of the crime."

"That's probably a good idea. Certainly couldn't hurt."

"Our unsub seems to know the dump scene well, so it must be someone that is familiar with the surrounding area. Could be a resident." He said that last part as if it left a bad taste in his mouth. "Or, it could be a well-seasoned visitor." He really did not want to admit that one of his islanders could be responsible for such a heinous act. "The only person of interest we have is that hippie fella. I know you said you don't think he did it, but he found her in a remote location hardly anyone goes to and on top of that, he had garbage bags because he just likes picking up trash on the sides of the road? Maybe he used the bags to carry her body out there, dumped her, and was taking them back with him so he didn't leave much evidence behind."

She had to admit that it he was a little odd, but her instincts were hardly ever wrong and she knew that man had nothing to do with it, other than finding the body. The bag was taken into evidence, they would have to wait for word of anything found.

"It just doesn't make much sense that he would've called it in if he had just dumped the body. I mean, if he really did it, and wanted her to be found, why not wait until he had left the area and call it in anonymously?" she pondered.

"Could be he is a narcissist and takes pride in his work, so to speak, and wanted to see the reactions from law enforcement and anyone else who happened to be there."

Valerie suddenly felt a shadow fall across her body from behind and the detective raised his eyes above her head.

"Good afternoon Detective." Valerie turned slightly in her chair to catch a glimpse of a man wearing black slacks and a white shirt. Although the day was a scorcher, the shirt had long sleeves and buttoned to his neck. He was obviously talking to Detective Morris because he was looking directly at him.

"Good Afternoon Pastor. I would like you to meet a colleague of mine, Detective Valerie Mason. Valerie this is Pastor Anthony Cross." The man turned and stared directly into her eyes. She felt instant guilt for not having attended church in years.

The man certainly did not look like a pastor that would welcome people on Sunday morning. He was bald, wearing thick black-rimmed glasses and extremely creepy looking. His skin was covered with a thin sheen of sweat, but yet he was wearing that long sleeved shirt.

"Nice to meet you Detective." He extended his hand to shake and when she touched it, it was cold as ice. Cold hands mean a warm heart, her mom always used to say. The smile he gave her never touched the corner of his eyes to make it seem genuine though. Some men of the cloth were so rigid. She always liked the preacher she had in her hometown as a child. He always had a smile and a joke to tell at a moment's notice. He made everyone feel welcome in their small church. Dad was never a big believer, so they just stopped going altogether after her mom died.

"We've missed you and your lovely wife in church these past couple of weeks."

Blushing, Detective Morris said, "Yeah, sorry about that. Been kinda busy, you know."

Smiling, the pastor contested, "Now where would we be if the Lord was too busy for us?" Poor guy, Valerie though. The detective looked like a scolded schoolboy. "Hopefully we'll see you this Sunday?" he asked.

"Me and the misses will certainly try to be there." The pastor nodded his head and walked away.

"Your Pastor is just a little bit creepy." Val said in jest.

"He is not really our Pastor. He is the new Associate Pastor. Our Pastor is Donald Lockhart, a real fine man. I have known him and his family for quite a few years. Pastor Cross just fills in for him when he goes on trips. He is the reason we haven't been the last couple of weeks. Pastor Lockhart has been gone, and well, Pastor Cross has only been here a few months and has left a strange impression. His sermons always sound so rehearsed like he is reading from a script and without emotion. He is just not what we like in a pastor."

"I gotcha." Val knew from past experiences that all kinds of preachers, just like all kinds of other people existed. They were not all cut from the same cloth.

About that time, Mary Anne brought a steaming cheese pizza pie and set it on the table before them. She handed each of them a plate and told them to enjoy. Val took a fork and used it to lift the crust of a slice of pizza and grabbed it with her hand. She dropped it quickly on her plate. It was so hot it burned the tips of her fingers. She quickly stuck them against the cool glass of tea to relieve the heat. She took her fork and knife and cut a piece off the tip of the slice and put in her mouth after blowing on it a few times to cool it down.

"Ummmm. That is delicious," she tried saying with a mouthful.

"I won't say I told you so."

"I think you just did," she laughed.

The two of them, having discussed all they could at the moment based on the information they had, didn't say much as they ate the rest of their lunch. They both enjoyed the coolness of the restaurant and the chance to relax a bit. Once Valerie finished, she leaned back in her chair to give her stomach some space. She had really stuffed herself. If she were at home by herself she would unbutton her pants so she could breathe a little better. She glanced around the room and noticed the Pastor was leaving, but not before he glanced back at their table one last time. Her eyes caught his. There was indeed something strange about that man. After he walked out the door, she found herself relieved. What a strange reaction to have she thought, then put it out of her head, as Detective Morris asked her if she had enjoyed her lunch.

"Very much so. It was just like you described it. I am afraid we didn't leave much for your receptionist though."

"I'll order one to go and take it with me." He motioned for Mary Anne to come over.

His cell phone rang and he dug it out of his pocket. "Speak of the devil," he said as he looked at the caller ID. When he finished talking he told Valerie that the co-workers of a young woman named Ali Musgrave were concerned because she had not shown up for work today, and she never misses work and hasn't answered her phone. A friend rode to her apartment to check on her, but she wasn't at home either.

"Can we get the check and a personal size to go please," he asked the waitress. Val took out her wallet, and Detective Morris waved it away. "Oh no, lunch is on me."

"Well that is really nice. Thank you. Next time, I'll buy your lunch."

"My wife would skin me alive if she found out I ever let a young lady pay for a meal."

"She sounds really sweet, and old fashioned."

"She is my high school sweetheart. Been married 38 years this coming September."

"Wow. That is amazing, and almost unheard of these days. I hope to find that one day."

"When the right one comes along, you'll know."

"That's what they tell me..." she replied with a smirk.

"Hey, I was right about the pizza, I'm right about this too."

"I guess. We'll just have to wait and see about that."

Mary Anne arrived with the check and the Detective gave her the money then told her to keep the change. He had to wait for the other pizza to finish cooking, so they said their goodbyes. Val reminded him she would let him know as soon as she had heard anything from the coroner.

After being inside, the light was almost blinding when she stepped outside. She had to feel around in her purse to find her shades. Once she put those on she could then look for her keys. As she was digging around in her purse, she had the feeling of being watched. She quickly looked around and didn't see anyone around the outside of the building. She headed toward her truck and took another glance around.

Nobody.

Why was she feeling so jumpy? From lack of sleep maybe? She slid into the driver's seat, fastened her seatbelt, and then cranked the engine. She pulled out of the spot she was parked in and headed home. She never noticed that black sedan that followed her all the way out to US1. She turned right to go to Key West, but it turned left into a bank parking lot and went back the same way it had come.

Chapter 4

Lieutenant Reed Stone walked down the dock to the blue and white Marine Patrol boat tied up in one of the slips. He could see his partner was not here yet for their morning shift. He dropped the duffel bag he was carrying into one of the seats. While he was waiting on his partner to arrive, he decided to check the dash and see if he could find his shades. He was almost certain he had left them on board when they had returned from patrol yesterday in the late afternoon. The sun's reflection was bound to be brutal today if the brightness of the morning was any indication, he definitely needed them. Looking around the boat, they were right where he left them. He slid them on and sighed with relief. He stood there for a minute just looking around at the beauty before him in the harbor. He had always been, and always would be an island boy. Although he was born in Orlando, his family had moved down here when he was eight years old. They had come for a visit one summer after his grandparents had decided to make this their retirement home and his parents fell in love with the island and its people. They soon returned to Orlando to sell their house, pack their belongings and headed back down here, which he thought was a gutsy move considering the fact that they had two kids to worry about taking care of. Together his parents and grandparents bought a small restaurant in Key West and made quite a nice living off the tourists that frequented the islands all year long and the residents who had come to love the food and atmosphere of the place. His life was a fantasy most people only dreamed of, and here he was living it out day by day. It wasn't just paradise to him, it was home.

~ ~ ~

His grandparents passed away several years ago within a few months of each other, a testament to their love and not wanting to live without the other. They left their house on Angela Street to him and his older brother, but Jason had moved away years ago to go to college at the University of Miami, then decided to take an apartment in Ft. Lauderdale after he graduated, so he didn't want or need the house. He signed his part over to Reed with the promise he would always have a place to stay when he came for a visit. Reed knew he would never leave here to live elsewhere, so he went to the Police Academy and then took a job with the Sherriff's Office Marine Unit.

He walked over to the duffel bag he had brought aboard and dug through it for some sunscreen. Pulling it out he began to spray it on his arms and legs. He sprayed some in his hands and rubbed his neck, tops of his ears and finally his face. He had to remove the shades he had just put on to rub the sunscreen on his face and in doing so, he caught the glare of sunlight on glass. He looked up at the colorful row of houseboats that lined one part of Garrison Bight Marina. Just yesterday as he had scanned the neat little line of pretty floating houses, he had spotted a gorgeous woman stepping out of a pair of sliding glass doors on the top deck of a porch. He wondered if she would be back out there this morning. She had long black hair that ended in soft curls around her shoulders and was wearing a next to nothing pale blue silk robe that fell halfway down her thighs. The front tied together but was gaping enough at the top exposing an enticing shot of cleavage. She watered her hanging plants and then put the watering can down on the side rail and picked up a cup of coffee. She turned to the rail and leaned against it raising the cup to her mouth. He thought she had to be the most beautiful woman he had seen in a very long time, and if she looked this good from this distance, what would it be like to see her up close? She must have sensed his staring because she turned and looked straight at him. Feeling his face turn red because he had been caught, he quickly looked away. He could still see her in his peripheral vision and she pulled the front of her robe together and walked back through the sliding glass doors pulling them closed behind her. If she saw him out here today, she would probably wait until he left to come back outside.

"She probably thinks I'm a creep," he muttered.

"I think you're a creep!" The voice of his partner Enrique Sotolongo, or Rick as he preferred to be called, caused him to jump.

"Damn it man, don't sneak up on me like that!"

Chuckling Rick replied, "What are you so grumpy this morning, and who thinks you're a creep?"

"I'm not jumpy, I just wasn't expecting anyone to come up behind me."

"Dude, you're a cop, you should expect the unexpected and besides that, I am supposed to be here, it's 7:00 and time to go to work."

"Shut up smart ass! It's too early in the morning for your b.s.," Reed said with a smile to let Rick know he was teasing. It wasn't necessary though because they had worked together for 8 years and knew each other's moods and sense of humor.

"Grouch. Sorry that someone pissed in your corn flakes this morning."

"Yeah, yeah. Crank her up and let's go."

"Whatever you say L-T. Where are we headed?"

"Take us out to the northern side of Cudjoe Key. We received reports of illegal lobster traps."

The old timers in the area felt that they should not have to have a permit to trap. Their families had fished these waters for years and felt that it all belonged to them. Reed secretly agreed, but it was illegal, and it was his job to enforce the law.

The water was as smooth and flat as glass this morning and in the distance, the sky was a beautiful watercolor of pinks, yellow, oranges and blues. The only thing better than sunrise in the Keys was sunset. It was indescribably magnificent. With a day as nice as today, he was feeling lucky to have a job that allowed him to be out in the water enjoying the view.

Up ahead, he could see a couple of boats anchored off the shore of a small island that really had no official name. It was between Sugarloaf Key and Cudjoe but was not inhabitable. It was a little odd that these boats would be gathered here at this time of the morning. There were small islands spread throughout the Keys that people gathered at to party, like Picnic Island where the water is shallow and clear like a swimming pool. Everyone puts down anchor and swims, or drifts on floats and generally just enjoys the water and sun while hanging out with friends. This, however, was not one of those spots. It was not known for fishing, and it had a rough shoreline with sharp rocks. Not to mention all the mangroves, small trees that appear as if they are on stilts standing up out of the water. This was not an ideal spot for much of anything.

Being spotted by a passenger in one of the boats, they were flagged towards the group. It was full of younger men who looked like they were heading out for a day of fishing.

"Can we help you gentlemen?" Rick asked as they pulled the boat up alongside of them and cut the engine. All at once several men started talking. Rick held up his hand "One at a time guys. We can't understand if everyone is talking at once."

"Sorry," one fisherman apologized. "We tried to call 911, but we couldn't get a signal out here. My buddy Tim here swears he saw an arm sticking up out of the water over there. We tried to get as close as we could to look, but it seems to have gone under or disappeared or something." He said pointing to a younger man that looked as if he was in his early twenties and was sitting on the front seat of the boat looking a little shook up. "We all looked and we all saw the same thing. Then it was just like it disappeared again."

Rick looked at Reed with a what-do-you-want-to-do look. Reed spoke up, "One of us will have to get in the water and go over there."

"Your call boss!" Rick waited for Reed's decision.

"Shit!" Reed muttered under his breath. He did not relish the thought of going in the water if there was a dead body in it.

"Guess I am going in," he sighed with resignation. He removed his gun belt from his shorts and unclipped his radio, took off his shirt and shades and put on a facemask and snorkel. He walked over to the ladder on the back of the boat, stepped over the ledge and jumped into the water feet first. It felt good, but it was disturbing knowing what else could be in there with him, and that thought made him shiver slightly. He swam about twenty-five yards or so from the boat to the mangroves the fishermen had pointed out.

He saw nothing. "Is this the spot?" he yelled across the water to them.

"Yeah, right in front of you!" one of them responded, pointing to a small cluster of mangroves.

As carefully as he could, he maneuvered around in the water so as not to disturb the sand on the bottom. He could see nothing so far which only meant he had to go under. Great, he thought as he pulled the mask over his face and took a deep breath, opting not to use the snorkel. He dipped down below the water. It was a little murky around mangroves. The roots of the trees were a perfect place for small marine life and the waves often times would keep the bottom stirred up in water this shallow. He slowly moved his arms to propel his body through the water and turned his head looking around. He saw nothing. He felt relieved. He surfaced and swam back to the patrol boat. Climbing up the ladder, he told them he couldn't find anything.

"Are you sure?" one of the boaters asked.

"Yeah, we know we weren't seeing things. Hell none of us have even had a beer this morning," one of the other men said with a chuckle that brought about snickering from a few of the others.

"Sir, I am not saying you didn't see it, but I can't find anything. If someone, or something is here, maybe, they will wash up on shore somewhere eventually, Reed said trying to not to show frustration at wasting his time here on men that had no doubt had a few already or maybe had not stopped from the night before, but were scared to admit it. Drinking and boating was just as serious as drinking and driving.

"Okay." The fisherman named Tim sounded deflated. "Guess we will keep an eye out in case we see anything else"

"That's about all you can do," Reed reassured. He then took some information from the group including names and phone numbers in case anything came up. He handed them a card with his name, badge number and phone number to the station should they find anything else. Rick started the engine and pulled slowly away from the other boats. He exchanged looks with Reed and lifted his eyebrows in an I-don't-know-what–to believe manner. Reed just shrugged his shoulders. He would write a brief report when he got back to the station. Like he had told the fishermen, it was all he could do. At least if anything turned up, they would have a record of someone reporting it. He kept going over it in his head. What could they have seen that made them think it was a human arm? Maybe it was a piece of driftwood that had a very convincing shape to it. Who knew?

What a way to start the morning. Good thing he had brought his thermos of sweet tea. He had a feeling caffeine would be his best friend today. He threw the clipboard with all the info he had taken from the fishermen into a storage box and took a big gulp of tea. Now, on to investigate the lobster traps that they had to set out to check on earlier.

Chapter 5

After reporting back to her station, finishing up some paperwork, then making several stops which included the grocery store and the bookstore who had ordered a special edition of The Old Man and the Sea for her, Val drove over the Palm Avenue Bridge in Key West and to her right could see Garrison Bight. Home sweet home. This particular marina harbored her yellow and white trimmed houseboat. The Marina was home to very unique and brightly painted floating houses, and was often a destination for tourists wanting to see one of the many unique lifestyles of the Florida Keys.

She loved living on the water. She fell into a great deal when the original owners wanted to be closer to a hospital because the husband was battling cancer and having some rare difficulties.

It was a two story "double-decker" and was perfect for her. The bottom floor housed a spacious living room that included a gas fireplace, which was rarely needed but nice to have, and the kitchen/dining area. The upstairs was the bedroom/bath, and a small room she used as a den all of which were more than large enough for a single woman. Each level had French doors that opened up to reveal ample porches. Both were covered in hanging baskets of various ferns and flowers and the top porch had a swing on one end where laziness reared its head more often than not. She loved her plants and hoped someday to have a regular garden with vegetables as well as flowers, but this would do for now.

There was space to entertain, but she rarely did that. She had only a few close friends and actually preferred solitude most of the time. It did not bother

her at all to stay home on a Friday or Saturday night when the bars and restaurants in Key West town were boiling over with people all out for a good time. She was just as happy settled in on her couch and reading a good novel than she would be partying the night away. Ernest Hemingway was her favorite writer and she had spent countless hours being entertained by him. She had to admit it was a little ironic now that she was living in Key West, and often wondered if it had influenced her to move here. She was almost sure it had to be a factor in her decision.

She had been to his house numerous times on Whitehead Street in Old Key West, just to walk around and explore the home and gardens trying to get a feel for what he must have been like. She had read countless tales of him penned by people who knew him, but those didn't always tell the real story, just their opinion of him.

Few people knew her well outside of work and the few close friends she had, she actually met at work.

Wow, that was a revelation even to herself. She knew she should venture out some, that there was more to life than work, but her interests just didn't fall into the category of bar hopping.

She was weary to the bone and longed for a cool refreshing shower. She had not slept much the night before and the heat of the day had physically drained her. She dropped her purse and bag with her case files in it on the couch and walking into the kitchen, she put her shopping bags down. She had gone in for coffee creamer and came out with bags full of junk. Opening the fridge she placed the creamer on the top shelf and grabbed a bottle of water. Holding it against her neck for a moment she leaned back against the coolness of the stainless steel appliance and sucked the whole bottle down in just a few gulps. Waiting for a few seconds, she pushed herself up out of the leaning position, threw the bottle into the recycle bin, and finished putting the groceries away.

Glad that was done for another week, she walked over and climbed the spiral staircase that took her upstairs and into her bedroom. The shades were drawn so her room had stayed relatively cool today. That, coupled with the fact there was very little light filtering in because of the rain clouds that were threatening, even from the skylight overhead, she debated lying down on the bed but knew if she did, she would be done until morning.

She walked on through to the bathroom and turned the shower on. Adjusting the hot water just enough to take the chill out of it, she peeled off her clothes that were so nice and crisp this morning and stepped into the water. It felt like pure liquid bliss. She let the water run over her neck and shoulders helping to ease away the tensions of the day. It felt so good that she couldn't understand why people often took so many little things for granted ... like a cool shower.

Her thoughts drifted to the girl that had been found that morning and she sighed deeply. Would she ever reach a point when she would no longer worry it might be her sister? Life is funny in the way that the events that shape our lives affect some of us positively and has a negative effect on others. Her mother's death, when she and her sister were just children, had been one of those events. It made Valerie determined to right the wrongs of the world so she became a police detective.

Her sister was another story, and quite the opposite. Breanna started giving their dad trouble in her early teens and had not backed off since, even though she was 27 years old now. She just wanted to grab her sometimes and shake some sense into her, to tell her to grow the hell up. She had been in trouble with the law off and on with shoplifting and underage drinking as a teen and God only knows what she was doing as an adult. She had run away countless times as a kid, and would leave now without telling anyone where she was going for days and sometimes weeks at a time. She would always come back though, when she hit rock bottom, or had nowhere to stay because her current boyfriend had kicked her out. Her sister always had an excuse for her behavior and loved playing the blame game. She loved blaming everyone else for her problems, especially their parents.

Dad didn't love mom enough.

Mom drank too much.

Valerie was the perfect child and could do no wrong.

She had heard them all over and over again. Not once did Breanna ever take responsibility for herself or her actions.

The memory of "the night" that threw her family's world into a tailspin began to play itself back in her head. Would she ever get to a point when she would go a day without thinking about it?

She remembered her parents having an argument that morning before her dad left for work about her mother's drinking the previous evening at a neighborhood BBQ, so it didn't help when he called later that afternoon and informed her that he would be late coming home from work.

"You're always late. What's you excuse this time?" she barely asked above a whisper, but Valerie heard her anyway. "Yeah, I'm sure it can't," her mother said, a little louder this time, responding to whatever her father had said on the other end. "The girls and I will find something else to do even though you promised to take them to movies." With that, she abruptly hung up the phone. She looked so tired, as if she needed to lie down and take a nap. She was quiet for a few minutes and wiped the corners of her eyes. "Put your shoes on girls. We are going to the movies." She managed a half smile.

"But mama, Daddy isn't home yet."

"No matter, it will be fun. Just us three, we'll have a girl's night out. Now go grab your sandals and let's go." She said with as much enthusiasm as she could muster.

The two ran off to find their shoes. They were so excited in those last few moments at the house. Now Val could go to school talking about the blockbuster hit Aladdin that all her friends had seen. Little did she know, they would never make it to the theater that night to see the movie about a boy and his friendship with a big genie and a little monkey. To this day, she could not bring herself to watch it.

The water from the rainfall showerhead mingled with the salty tears than ran down her cheeks. She wondered if she would ever be able to put it all behind her and move on. Sometimes she thought that was the reason she preferred solitude. No commitments. Therefore no one could let her down. She knew in her head that she needed to move past that and open herself up to new things and people and just feel normal for once. Maybe one day she could, but right now, she just wanted to fall into bed and sleep and let all the troubles of the world float away.

She turned off the faucets and grabbed a towel, quickly wrapping her hair in one and grabbed another to wrap her body in. She decided against blow-drying her hair out. It would be wild and unruly in the morning, but at this point she didn't care. She though briefly about making a sandwich, but decided sleep was a bigger priority, and after her lunch today with Detective Morrison, she wasn't really that hungry.

After brushing her teeth, she walked back in to her room and lay down on the bed. Looking up she could see the sky through the amazing skylight that was just above her bed. It was one of the selling points for her when buying her house.

It was getting ready to rain, judging by the dark clouds and the flashes of lightening that lit up an otherwise darkening room every couple of minutes. The thunder could be heard rumbling in the distance and she knew this was the storm she had seen earlier today rolling towards them across the vast expanse of the sea. She lost all sense of time staring up at the sky and could feel her body slowly relaxing. Soon she was drifting off. Her last conscious thought was the pinging of the raindrops on the tin roof sounded like little bells playing a soft melody somewhere off in the distance. She was sound asleep before the rain started coming down in a torrential downpour.

~ ~ ~

Janine Brown sat at a corner table at the Blue Dolphin Pub alone. She was mulling over a decision and had promised herself that if she decided to go through with it, this would be it. The last time. After tonight she would never, under any circumstances, turn a trick again.

She had given up drugs 4 months ago and was proud of it. She hated herself for resorting to this to pay for her last class, but tuition was expensive and she couldn't get a job without finishing her class.

That was her life though. No silver spoon in her mouth as a babe. Her Grammie had raised her after her mom ran off with a trucker that had wanted her mother, but not with Janine in tow.

Good riddance! If that was the kind of woman her mother was, she didn't need her.

Her Grammie was a kind and loving woman who baked cookies and took her to church on Sunday, until she grew into an obstinate teen who refused to go. She started hanging out with the wrong crowd, and the rest, as they say, is history. She wanted to cry thinking of all the heartache she had caused her Grammie when all she had done was love Janine in return.

Taking a sip of her cola, she looked around. She caught a man who had been making eye contact for quite a while. She had been in the business long enough to recognize a mark when she saw one. He was well dressed and older than her. That made him a little creepy. Of course, she was only twenty-two, so she considered anyone over thirty older, and he was definitely over thirty.

He stood up and made his way over to her table.

"Nice night," he finally spoke.

"Sure" she said trying to convince herself not to go through with it, hoping he would just walk away.

"Are you here alone?"

"Yeah."

"I was just about to grab a bite to eat and to be honest, I don't like eating alone. I figured since you looked like you were alone also, you might want to share a meal."

"Sounds alright. There's a nice steak place on the next block."

"If that's what you'd like, I could go for a steak."

She stood up grabbing her purse from the seat next to her. He allowed her to walk in front of him as they headed towards the front. Once out the door and into the night, her destiny had been put in motion. She started towards the restaurant and he said, "I know a shortcut."

This would be her final trick after all.

What could have been a few minutes or a few hours later, she felt cold. She tried reaching down for her comforter, but realized that she was not in her bed. Her bed was soft, not hard like the surface she was lying on.

Why couldn't she move her arms and legs? There was something over her mouth too. She fought to open her eyes. It was as if there were lead weights on her eyelids holding them closed. She finally managed to get them to cooperate. She was lying on her back staring up a ceiling that had only a naked bulb hanging from a broken light fixture.

Looking around at the bare room she thought she was in some sort of shed. It wasn't much bigger than a shed anyway. Only one door in and out. All the windows except one had been boarded up. Fear began to seize her heart and she had to fight the urge to vomit. There was tape across her mouth so if she did throw up, she could choke on it.

The previous night came flooding back in flashes. The realization she had been kidnapped by the older man at the bar brought bile to the back of her throat again. Quickly, she pushed it down.

If only she hadn't needed that money. She should have tried to get a part time job at a fast food chain, or cleaning hotel rooms instead old resorting to her old life of turning tricks. Just once more she had promised herself, and look what that one more time has gotten her. Now her thoughts were being tortured by what-ifs and regrets of leaving the pub with that man, but too late now. It was over and she had nobody but herself to blame.

STOP IT she told herself. You have survived a lot of shit in life and you can find a way out of this too, you just gotta keep your head. She had never been in a situation quite this bad, although she had to run away from her pimp in Daytona Beach several years ago, and dealers from Miami she owed money to. The fear kept trying to creep back. Out of the silence, she could have sworn she heard her Grammie's voice.

"PRAY."

She hadn't done that in years. What good would it do? She was an ex-junkie and a prostitute and was quite sure that God wrote her off a long time ago, or had she been the one to write him off? Either way it didn't matter. She knew he wasn't likely to listen to someone like her. Maybe she should have talked to one of the preachers that were always stopping by the women's shelter offering assistance and counseling.

She could hear the rumbling of thunder in the distance. Maybe she could figure out where she was by listening for any sounds coming from outside. The faint sounds of vehicles could be heard so she must be close to some type of roadway. There was also water close by if what she was hearing was the sound of water lapping softly against a shoreline, but then again this was an island, unless he had taken her somewhere on the mainland.

All at once, she heard a sound that seemed to suck the air out of the atmosphere. It was an eerie whistle. Someone was whistling a familiar tune from the recesses of her memory.

When she was small, and lived with Grammie, she remembered her humming this tune, sometimes singing the words, as she sat in her rocker on the front porch shelling peas or peeling potatoes. It was something about gathering together at a river.

Now would be a good time for that prayer, she thought she heard her Grammie say.

Our Father, who art in Heaven, Hallowed be thy name.

The whistling was getting closer.

They kingdom come, thy will be done ... please let it be your will for me to get out of here.

On earth as it is in heaven.

... closer

Give us this day our daily bread and forgive us...

The door lock rattled making her forget the last part of that verse.

Lead us no into temptation ... I'm sorry, I know I screwed that part up real bad. Deliver us from evil ...

The door was unlocked and being opened.

For thine is the kingdom, the power, and the glory forever and ever... Amen her mind screamed.

The door opened fully, and the evil she had prayed for deliverance from, stepped inside.

~ ~ ~

The rain was pounding so loud it sounded as if the roof would collapse from the weight of it. He covered his ears with his hands. He never had liked the rain, especially the thunder and lightning. He could feel a dull ache beginning behind his eyes and knew that before the night was over, something bad would happen as it always did when the headaches came. He didn't know why he did what he did, and that is what bothered him most. He was very analytical and wanted a reason for everything, and would often question everything as a child, like most children do, that would send his mother into a lethal rage. She punished him severely every time he broke one of her precious rules, or asked the wrong thing, while the sorry excuse that called himself father stood by and let her do it. Once his dad had tried to stop her, but mother turned the belt around and hit him right across the face with it. Father walked out that night and did not come back for an entire week. Mother softened some in that week thinking he was gone for good. Not because she cared, that was something she could not do for anyone other than herself.

Father was her meal ticket, with the amount of money he had inherited after his father died. Without him she would be destitute. She didn't even care about the other women he spent his time with even though she would preach to the boy about women with loose morals. When his father returned, she told him over and over again how truly sorry she was and it would never happen again. Father was told he shouldn't interfere when she was trying to punish the boy for his naughty behavior, afterwards locking him in his room until she was sure that he had repented and had been forgiven. Maybe that was why he felt as if he were specifically ordained from God to punish the sinful and unchaste. He was following in his mother's footsteps. He had been "saving" women since his early teens, disposing of their bodies where they could not be found. But lately, the idea of letting the world know what he was doing was becoming more and more fascinating. It would give the message that people needed to turn from their immoral ways before it was too late. He was doing the Lord's work, so he made certain that before they closed their eyes for the last time, and stood before the judgment seat of their maker, their soul had been cleansed.

He heard whimpering behind him. Turning, he could see the pitiful creature that needed to be released from this world of sin. He had found her sitting at a pub all alone in Key West enticing men to have wicked and lustful thoughts about her with the way she was dressed. He had to act like one of the men who frequented these places cheating on their wives, and fornicating with these vile creatures who disguised themselves as pretty women. When you got up close to them, you could tell it was only make up that made them look halfway attractive. They were haggard, drained, and shattered by the hand that life had dealt them and the lives they had lived because of it. He convinced this particular one to take a walk with him, promising her a quiet dinner at a pricey restaurant just down the street. Of course, she had fallen for it. He was a decent looking man dressed in nice clothes that were higher end. He was always careful to wear a disguise so people would not easily recognize him.

Women like her always dreamt of a better life, and would do anything for a man willing to give it to her. Once he had her alone, he convinced her to go down an alley as a shortcut.

The silly girl thought he wanted to have sex with her in that vermin-infested side street. The smell of vomit and urine was enough to make him gag. She smiled seductively and ran her hand up and down his back. The touch made him feel even more nauseous. He would never be with this woman as tarnished as she was! He forced himself not to act repulsed and smiled at the thought of what was really about to befall her. She thought he was smiling at her offer, and walked ahead of him swinging her hips back and forth in an exaggerated manner until she came to the end of the alley and turned around and leaned back against the wooden fence that separated the alley from the back of a private residence. He walked towards her and working quickly, acted as if he was going to wrap his arms around her in a hug. Instead he palmed the small hypodermic needle he had taken from his pocket, being careful not to stick himself. She was reaching up to put her arms around his neck and that's when he struck. Right above her elbow he stuck the needle in and pushed the plunger.

"Owwww, you asshole! What did you just do?" she yelled trying to twist her arm and look at her elbow. Her vision was already starting to blur and her tongue was beginning to feel thick. She realized now that she had been drugged and this psycho was probably going to rape her and leave her for dead in this alley. The man in front of her remained silent grabbing her by the arm to support her as she felt her knees beginning to buckle. A bright light from the house behind the fence snapped on. It was the last thing she saw before losing consciousness.

Now, here she lay trying to clear her mind from the hazy fog induced state she was in. She stared at him with her eyes wide and filled with fear and shock. He gave her a small comfort by patting her on the head.

"There, there child." He tried to comfort all those he helped, because comfort is the one thing he had never received from anyone after being punished. "Now, calm down. Soon all the misery you have known in this life will be over and you will be cleansed of mind, body and soul. The despicable things you are guilty of will be forgiven and you will only know peace."

None of this of course brought any comfort, it just managed to terrify her all the more especially when recognition of who he really was finally hit her. She had seen him at the women's shelter, and now that he had removed his fake mustache, she could clearly see him for who he really was. She struggled against the tape that bound her hands and feet, as well as held the gag in her mouth. She watched as he stood up and removed the belt he was wearing around his waist. At first, he saw the flash of fear that comes when a woman thinks a man is about to sexually assault her. He folded both ends of the belt around each of his hands and knelt down beside her and placed it against her throat. Her eyes could not have grown any larger without popping out of her head. She had reached the only other conclusion she could. She was sobbing uncontrollably now, but the gag and duct tape over her mouth prevented any discernible screams from escaping. She started thrashing her head back and forth, but was still weak from the drugs he had injected into her arm earlier.

Pushing as hard as he could against the struggling woman he started speaking to her. The last words she heard were "He will wipe away every tear from their eyes, and death shall be no more, there will no longer be any mourning, crying, or pain." before the sound of her own heart pounding in her ears drowned out everything else, and at last there was nothing but darkness and silence.

Chapter 6

Valerie stretched her arms above her head and felt her body slowly come awake. Glancing at her alarm clock on the nightstand, she yawned as she read the bright red numbers 6:35. She had finally had a good night's sleep and felt fully rested. No nightmares plagued her last night as they sometimes did. She quickly pushed those thoughts away.

She must not have moved all night long from the position she fell asleep in, because she was on her back with the towel still wrapped partly around her hair. Sitting up, she pulled it off and threw it across the room.

Her stomach rumbled reminding her that she had not eaten anything since lunch yesterday. Sitting up on the edge of the bed, her towel wrapped around her torso fell open. She had been so tired she hadn't even put on pajamas last night. She stood up and walked over to her dresser to grab a T-shirt and panties to put on temporarily until she had eaten and was ready to get dressed for work.

Walking down the stairs, she ran her fingers through her hair and feeling multiple tangles, sighed. She gave bed head a whole new meaning.

She grabbed a coffee mug out of the cabinet. Walking over to her one serving coffee maker and placing the cup underneath, she picked up a strong Jamaican blend coffee pod, dropped it in, and pushed the on button. She had just bought the coffee maker a few months ago. She rarely drank more than one cup a day in the heat, so it worked perfectly for her. She had a regular coffee maker for those rare cool days when she could drink more than one cup or even rarer occasions when she had company. Delaney was really the only friend she ever had over.

She walked over to the couch where she had dropped her messenger bag last night. She used it to carry all her case files, and after picking up her cup of coffee, she took a seat at the table. She spread what little information she had out on the tabletop needing to organize it all. Later she would drive down to the Coroner's building in Marathon and see if Delaney had started the autopsy yet. Maybe she had finished already. Not likely, but here's hoping, she thought. Probably an open and shut case. It could be domestic violence, being in the wrong place at the wrong time, or a drug deal gone wrong. None of which were uncommon these days, but something felt off about it.

Needing to check her department email to see if any of the pictures taken at the scene yesterday had been forwarded to her, she reached into her bag and took her laptop out, and turned it on. Naturally, the battery was almost dead. She dug around in her bag for the cord and pulling it out, then plugged it in. She logged into her department site by clicking on the icon on the desktop and scrolled down to find the one for email. Scanning through the new and unread she found one with the subject CS174 on 6/26/17 – PHOTOS. Now she had something to work with. It also reminded her to call Al Foster to get a copy of the pictures he had taken.

Glancing at the clock on the stove, she still had an hour before she had to be at the station. That would give her enough time to look over the photos while finishing her coffee and getting dressed for work. The station was not very far. It only took her a few minutes to get there. Besides, she was always early. She had never been late for the reasons everyone else seemed to have like an early morning lovers rendezvous or wrestling with kids to get them ready for school. Good grief, what had her life become? Even she could see how pathetic she was.

Looking back down at the computer, she thought it was time to get off the pity train and get to work. The computer was taking its sweet time downloading the pictures so she got up to make a piece of toast. She grabbed the homemade cinnamon apple jelly her Dad had given her on her last trip home, and a butter knife out of the drawer. The toast popped up and she spread the pretty light red jelly on it and plopped back down in her chair at the table.

She noticed that two photos had downloaded so she clicked on the first one. Poor soul, was her first thought. She made several notes based on the picture to ask Delaney including a question about the gold bracelet the girl was wearing. She wanted to see if it has anything inscribed on it or perhaps fingerprints. Since there was no purse or ID found at the scene, it might be the one of the few things that could lead to her identification. She also made a note to call the Missing Persons Unit to see if anyone fitting the girl's description had been reported missing lately. Detective Morris had received a call yesterday from a concerned co-worker of a young woman who had missed work, and was checking into it as a possible missing person.

Several other pictures were finished downloading and needed to be opened, but they would have to wait. Time was growing short so she took her cup to the sink and rinsing it out along with the plate, she placed them in the dishwasher. She returned to the table and picked up her files and laptop, stuffing them into her bag and then headed upstairs to get dressed. She had a nagging suspicion this case was not going to be as cut and dried as it seemed, and wanted to get started on it.

She pulled out a pair of khakis and a green lightweight pullover with the sheriff's department insignia embroidered on it to wear. Trying to keep her wardrobe as light as possible because of the heat, she was glad her uniform days were over with. That polyester blend that they were made of was every Floridian's nightmare.

She quickly brushed her hair back and pulled it into a high ponytail. She sighed at her reflection in the mirror but this was as good as it was going to get this morning. A quick coat of mascara then brushing her teeth, and she was ready to meet the day.

Once outside, sweat started to form on her forehead reminding her that she wasn't looking forward to traipsing around outside today. She hoped all the answers she needed would be found lying in the autopsy room.

Yeah, she thought, you just keep on with that wishful thinking, Val, just keep wishing.

~ ~ ~

Delaney stood at the deep sink in the autopsy room scrubbing her hands. Patting them dry she pulled on a pair of surgical gloves and walked over to the young woman lying on the cold metal table waiting for her to discover all the answers the police needed to catch a killer. Her assistant Eric O'Shay had the day off, and she had come in early to get started. She liked to get here ahead of everyone else so she had time to work undisturbed. Since Eric wouldn't be in, she had to gather all her instruments and the things she might need, and once arranged on the tray beside the table, she stepped towards the examination table.

"Here's hoping for the results that will get you some justice, kiddo," she said aloud.

She had bagged her clothes and shoes earlier so she reached up and turned on the overhead microphone to record all her findings starting with the date and time. She named the victim as a Jane Doe until her identity could be established, and noted her height to be five foot four inches, weighing 120 lbs. Her shoulder length hair was blond and had been highlighted with black streaks and bangs.

Starting with the visual exam of the body, she carefully searched her skin for cuts or abrasions. She noted there was sticky residue around the mouth, wrists and ankles, and a red discoloration indicative of being bound by some sort of tape. She took a comb and pulled it slowly through her hair for any trace that might be clinging there and carefully placed the comb and the findings in an evidence bag noting the case number on it. Examining the hands and fingernails were next. There was not much trace under the nails but she bagged what little there was anyway. The nails were all normal with none being broken or having jagged edges. Her arms or hands did not appear to have any defensive wounds indicating there was not much, if any struggle.

Upon closer examination of the left arm, she noticed the tiniest bruise at the top of the left elbow. She pulled the expandable magnifier towards the bruised area and noted the mark to be a perfectly round penetrating wound in what looked to be a needle mark. It was just the right size to be that of a 26-gauge syringe. She checked both arms then to see if she could find tracks that would indicate drug use, but there were none. Perhaps she had found the way the killer subdued her and if so, this is why there were no defensive wounds. She knew to be very careful to take plenty of samples for the toxicological reports. Following her notations on the needle mark, she used a rape kit to collect evidence, though there were no visual signs of trauma. If she had a boyfriend or spouse who was responsible for her death, this could give them a clue to his identity and then eventually, her identity through him.

The internal exam came next with her beginning by making a Y incision from shoulder to shoulder, down the breastbone all the way to the top of her pubic bone. She collected evidence from blood to stomach contents that were all put in the proper specimen collections cups and bags to send off for further analysis. She checked to see if the girl had breast implants which she didn't. Often times the serial number on implants could be used to identify victims. No such luck here. This young lady was well endowed naturally. She continued on by checking and weighing all the organs and noting their conditions. Her heart was healthy and there were no signs of smoking. Her liver showed no signs of excessive drinking. She was living pretty clean for someone so young these days, especially in the environment of the Florida Keys bars and partying.

Finally came the last part of the exam, which was the head. She could see petechial hemorrhaging in the eyes which told her the girl had either been hanged or strangled. There were visible bruises around her throat that were approximately an inch wide and rectangular. Her best guess would be a belt or some kind of strap, so the natural conclusion was strangulation. She checked the hyoid bone and noted it was broken, which was a strong indicator along with the eye hemorrhaging, that the victim has been strangled. It took a lot of strength to strangle someone to death, so more than likely the killer was a man. There were no other signs of trauma to the head.

Delaney finished up by stitching the victim back up and then covering her with a white sheet. She took her time making her stitches even like it was going to matter to this young girl who had the perfect figure. She always felt a little sad knowing she was the last human contact a person would have other than the funeral director, but it was all part of the job. She couldn't dwell on it too much or it would drive her crazy. At least through her work, families could get closure, most of the time anyway. She double checked all her samples and reports for accuracy and signed off on them. The only thing left was the death certificate and releasing the body. Since they had no idea who she was and no next of kin to notify yet, she would hold off signing the death certificate until the toxicology reports came back. She was sure the COD was strangulation, but wanted to make sure that the needle mark she had found was not the real cause. She was determined to do her part to bring this young girl's killer to justice.

She had just sat down at her desk when she heard the buzzer at the front door ring. There was only one person she could think of that would be here this early. She smiled and went over the monitor to confirm her suspicions and ring her in.

~ ~ ~

Val parked in one of several parking spots outside the building that served as the coroner's office. The only other car in the lot was Delaney's red Miata. She picked up the small carrier containing two lattes and headed for the front door. She pushed the button on the call box next to the door and waved at the camera in the corner above the door. Normally the door remained unlocked, but since Delaney was here alone because she had come in early, she couldn't blame her for being cautious. You just never knew these days what crazy things people would try.

Once inside, Val walked down a hallway past the business office and then left down another short hallway. Pushing the square chrome button with the emblem of a hand on it, the door swung open with a quiet swoosh. Val saw Delany sitting at her desk in the back corner of the room.

"Hey you," Delaney greeted her.

"Good morning. I hope you're in need of refreshment. I stopped at the Donut Hole for lattes."

"I am so thankful for the caffeine that I'll keep my cop and doughnut shop joke to myself."

"Gee, thanks," Val said with a smile.

Taking a big sip of the steaming latte Delaney asked Val, "How are things going?"

"That's why I'm here."

"Not with the investigation, with you."

"I was afraid that's what you meant. You know me, work, work, work!"

"Yes, I do know you, which means you have been spending all your free time at home alone reading Hemingway or spending time at his house hoping to see his ghost so you can discuss all the important things in life with him. God! We need to find you a real man!"

"I do not hang around his house hoping to see a ghost. I don't believe in that sort of thing, and he *was* a real man," Val defended.

"You know what I mean. One that has a pulse. And one that is not old enough to be your great grandfather." Delaney said with a giggle causing Valerie to laugh too.

"When you put it like that it does sound ... weird," Val said searching for the right word.

"Rick and I are going to Palms Patio tomorrow night. Say you'll come with us," Delaney pleaded.

"I don't want to be a ..."

"Third wheel. I know you always say that, but he can bring a friend and then you won't feel awkward."

"Oh no, that would never be awkward!" her voice dripped with sarcasm.

"Please, for me? I'll even pay for your dinner."

Valerie had been thinking about how her life was becoming pathetic just this morning. Maybe it was time to get out and enjoy herself a little. "I'll think about it, but NO promises."

Delaney clapped her hands like a little girl.

"I said no promises!" Val reinforced.

"At least you're thinking about it, that is a huge step forward."

"Well let's get to the real reason I'm here, which has nothing to do with my social life, or the lack thereof."

Delaney turned and looked over at the autopsy table. She had not even returned the body to the cold storage locker. "I just finished her before you got here and haven't had time to write my report. I was starting it when you got here. I can email it to you this afternoon."

"That's ok. I prefer to hear it from you firsthand anyway. Your descriptions help me more than a generic form report." They both walked over to the table and Delaney pulled the sheet back to chest level. They both were quiet for a minute as they stared at a young life taken so soon.

"She was definitely strangled" Delaney said breaking the silence. "Her hyoid bone is broken and the bruises on her neck and throat area are the right size for a belt or similar object. Her eyes have petechial hemorrhaging, another indicator of strangulation. I am betting dollars to doughnuts your perp is a man because of the strength it takes to break a hyoid during strangulation. I think she may have been subdued by drugs of some kind. She has this needle mark here on her arm." Delaney pointed to the diminutive mark on the girls arm.

"Any clues to her identity?"

"None unfortunately. She had no previous surgical scars, no tattoos or birthmarks. She only had three fillings. She took really good care of her teeth."

"She was wearing a gold bracelet when she was found. Did you happen to get anything from it?"

"No. There was no inscription where one should be. You can try to lift prints from it to see what you can find. I have her prints that you can compare it to. I could find nothing to tell us who she is. I can compare dental records to her, if and when we get a hit on her ID.

"Damn. It's so sad. She is so young and pretty." Val thought about her sister who was just about the same age. Shaking that though off, she shivered slightly.

"You ok?"

"I'm fine. It just amazes the evil men do."

"I know what you mean. I see plenty of evil in here." They both were quiet again for several moments.

Trying to lighten the suddenly oppressive mood Delaney asked "So, about tomorrow night. Are you going?"

"I haven't even had time to think about it!" Val cried foul.

"Sure you have! Besides when you start thinking too much, it gets you in trouble."

Not feeling real sure, but wanting to have some fun and an evening out with her best friend, Val reluctantly agreed. "But under one condition!"

"Whatever you want." Delaney was willing to agree to almost anything to get her friend out for a night of fun and relaxation.

"This is not a blind date and you're not setting me up with one of Rick's friends."

"I promise I am not setting you up. I just don't want you to feel like you're a third wheel, as you like to put it, so there might be an extra person at the table. That's all."

Valerie must not have looked convinced because Delaney added holding her hand up "I swear on my grandma's grave."

Val rolled her eyes, "You're grandmother is not dead."

"One of them is!"

"Well for your sake, I hope you're telling the truth. Make sure you tell this extra person at the table I carry a gun for a living so he doesn't get any ideas."

They both laughed and made plans for what time to meet the next night, said goodbyes and Val headed out to see Detective Morris to share the results of the autopsy. Delaney laughed out loud after the door closed behind her friend. Little did Val know that the extra person at the table would be Rick's best friend, and he carried a gun for a living too.

Chapter 7

The day had begun with an oppressively humid temperature of 79°. It was certain to be another scorcher with temps like that at seven a.m.

Al Foster finished watering his plants around the edges of his patio that sat below his house on stilts. A large majority of the houses in the Keys were built up on stilts to prevent flooding and high water when there were storms. A brisk afternoon rainstorm could produce a deluge on these islands which were barely above sea level. Rising tides could be troublesome at times too, given the right conditions out in the ocean. The stilt houses provided beneficial shade and the extra outdoor living space that most people utilized it for. Even on the hottest of days, the ocean breeze could be felt moving under the houses and around the patio areas.

He walked down the brick path to the canal that ran directly behind his house. This is where he docked his boat, but he came out each day to peer into the water for small sea life. These canals were teeming with little underwater neighbors from lobster and octopi to beautiful multi colored angelfish. He was checking to see if the resident lobster had crawled out from under his rock ledge. The water was clear and still this morning, but the lobster was nowhere to be seen. There were dozens of Cassiopeia, the "upside down" jellyfish. A small octopus about the size of a half dollar was doing a lovely waltz about three feet below the surface. He thought them to be some of the most beautiful sea creatures in the ocean. He would check back later on the lobster. It was rather large and he wanted to get a couple pictures of it to show to some friends.

He turned and walked back up the brick path to the side of the house where he parked his island-wide recognizable trike. He wasn't going to ride to the Blue hole today. He was still shook up over finding that young girls body a couple of days ago. He shivered slightly despite the morning heat.

Today, he would take the nature trail to see if he could spot a pair of Bald Eagles he had taken many photos of, one of which ended up on an advertisement pamphlet for the nature preserve. His girlfriend, Beverly Gail, worked for the printing company that had made the pamphlets, so she presented Al's nature shots to her boss. He had thought them incredible and had asked for permission to publish them.

He rode the mile or so from his house to the entrance of the trail announced by a wooden sign. The words "Jack Watson Nature Trail" alongside a picture of Jack Watson himself carved into the sign, stood in remembrance of a man instrumental in the preservation of the land and its famous Key deer. It was one of the last wooded areas still in the keys. Progress had taken its toll in most of the islands.

The walk itself could take anywhere from thirty minutes to an hour depending on how brisk you walked, or how often you stopped to read the signs that explained what plants you were looking at. It wasn't a difficult walk, but was left as natural as possible, so the trail was just pea rock.

There was another small dirt trail leading off in another direction, on the other side of the road, but that one was off limits to the public. It was barricaded by a yellow locked gate, which was the dumbest thing he had ever seen. All one had to do was walk around it. There was no fence, but it did block vehicles from going down it though, so he guessed that was why it was there. The entrance was used by wildlife officers as a dumpsite when the deer were hit by careless drivers. The deer were taken to the back of the property and placed out where nature could reclaim them. You certainly did not want to be downwind of them when they had been out there a few days. Al figured those poor deer had provided more than a few meals for the eagles as well as other scavengers, which was probably the reason they were often present on this part of the island.

He made sure his camera strap was secure around his neck and took an expandable walking stick out of the basket on his bike. He pushed the button on the end allowing it to extend and started down the trail. He used it more as protection than anything else by poking around on the ground and in the bushes before walking through uncertain areas. He also used it to move the poisonwood back should he get close enough to come in contact with it. The sap from that particular tree could be bad news.

There were signs pointing it out along the trail to warn visitors. He ignored it at times and left the trail to do a little "hunting". There was no shortage of flora or fauna to take pictures of and he used it to his advantage. Friends had suggested that he publish a book of his photographs and he was considering it. He hadn't made any plans though, because it sounded too much like work, and he was retired. Period.

He looked for the beauty in the ordinary everyday things. There was so much to find if one took the time and effort to look. People found it through his pictures, often commenting on social media where he posted them for everyone to enjoy.

Signs were placed on the trail that explained the scenery and its plant life as well as the animals one might encounter along the way. Other signs stated: "Trails are closed beyond this point"

Beautiful yellow flowers named Big Pine Partridge Pea were a favorite of butterflies as well as the Butterfly Pea, a pale purple color aptly named for the little winged creatures that fluttered around it. Along with those were the long stalked toppers, a white flower with a feathery looking center and the Florida Whitetop. Each and every one was preserved forever in a photograph by Al.

Several mosquito ditches ran along part of the path. These were dug out in the 1960's to control the population of mosquitoes without having to use harmful chemicals.

Unfortunately, the ditches filled with salt water and dumped right into fresh water, making them drinking hazards for deer. Fawns were often found drowned in them after falling in trying to get a drink, so they started filling them in to protect the deer, but leaving them open just enough to control the mosquitoes.

It was as still as a Monday morning church without so much as a whisper of a breeze. The stillness meant the heat would be close to unbearable today. Some people would find their respite at the beaches, but Al was accustomed to it. His darkly tanned skin was a testament to the fact.

He heard a slight rustle in some brush nearby and stood very still. A small marsh rabbit came cautiously out onto the path and stopped. He raised the camera slowly, so as not to startle the little guy, and clicked off two pictures. Curiosity got the better of the rabbit so he raised up on his hind legs with his front paws hanging in front, his little nose twitching and sniffing the air. Al snapped two more shots before the rabbit dropped down on all fours and hopped off to the other side of the trail.

He decided to follow the rabbit. Maybe it would lead him to a little family. He had left the trail and gone about 20 yards, when the ground started to slightly give way. After all the rain they had the last couple of weeks, the ground was saturated and very mushy.

He saw the rabbit scamper around a palmetto and off to the right into a marshy area. He thought about following him further but had no desire to sink up to his knees in mud should the ground be worse than what it was where he was standing. He could smell a foul odor and could not tell if it was mud and rot from the wet vegetation or maybe a whiff of a dead deer coming from the back, but he was headed back to the main trail anyway. He would have to ride home with muddy feet and ankles. As he turned around to start back towards the trail, he caught something out of the corner of his eye. Something he prayed he would never see again.

~ ~ ~

Val decided to head to the doughnut shop this morning for breakfast before going in to the station. There was a corner booth in the back she sat in and could spread her work out if she needed to where no one would bother her.

The sound of her phone ringing startled her as she sat going over the autopsy notes that Delaney had emailed her. She saw it was Detective Morris. He had probably just received the same email and wanted to go over some of the details.

"Good morning, this is Detective Mason."

"Hello detective. I wish I could say good morning back. We got another body. It was found by the same fella that found the first one. A little too coincidental if you ask me."

"A little." She admitted. Surely her instincts could not have failed her about Al Foster, but then again … "I'm on my way in five minutes."

"Believe me, the poor thing is not going anywhere." He replied.

She hurried to put her things in the bag and threw a ten-dollar bill on the table and hurried out the door. She had parked the Explorer behind the building so she hurried around the side into an alleyway trying not to slosh her coffee. She had taken the lid off to cool it, and left it lying on the table.

She reached the explorer and had to put the coffee cup on the roof so she could get her keys out of the bag. Unlocking the truck, she threw her bag into the passenger seat and slammed the door. Damn! Opening the door she got back out to grab her coffee from the roof. Climbing back in and setting the coffee in the console cup holder, she cranked the ignition. Pulling carefully from the spot where she was paralleled parked, she thought about Al Foster. She had only met him once, but she did not get any bad vibes from him. Different vibes maybe, but not the kind to make you think the man was a killer. She would question him further when she saw him today.

She headed out of Key West towards Big Pine Key. The drive would take her no more than 30 minutes if the traffic was good. Being Thursday, it shouldn't be congested. Starting tomorrow, it would really turn into a nightmare.

To arrive at the new scene, she had to pass the old one. It was slightly down the road but this crime scene was very reminiscent of the last one. Onlookers were being held back by yellow crime scene tape. Several officers were standing watch and calming residents.

The coroners van was parked over to the side with the back doors open, and a white haired man sitting on a multi-color trike was filling out what she assumed was another statement. The only difference this time was the presence of the media. There were only two vans bearing different station names on the sides, but that meant two reporters would want answers.

As she stepped out of the truck, she could hear one of the reporters call out to her. She ignored him and kept her eyes averted towards the distance. Walking quickly towards the crime scene tape she could hear the other reporter in an oh-so-reporter like voice saying, "In what is normally a paradise for residents and tourists alike, something dark and dangerous has come to the islands."

Dramatic much, she thought, shaking her head. The first reporter was still trying to speak and question any cop that would oblige. So far there was no one.

Detective Morrison was standing off to the side with Al Foster guarding him as if he was suddenly going to make a break for it on the three-wheeler, and the burly old detective would have to give chase. He was gunning for Mr. Foster to be the main suspect and was probably contemplating taking him in so he could stick him under a hot light and beat him with a rubber hose. This made Val smile, but she had to quickly wipe it away because this was not the appropriate time or place for her quirky sense of humor.

She parked on the side of the road and climbed out. Detective Morris noticed her and waved her over. Mr. Foster gave her a small smile, but there was no humor in it. She returned it with the same and a slight wave.

"Mr. Foster, you are either the unluckiest man on this island, or you have a knack for finding dead bodies. Maybe we should put you on the payroll."

"Believe me detective, I wish it had been anybody other than me. I haven't quite recovered from the first."

"Yet, here we are again," she said solemnly.

Detective Morris cleared his throat. "I told Mr. Foster we may need him for further questioning, so not to go too far."

"I have no plans to Detective. I know how this must look, but I swear, I had nothing to do with this."

"Ok, Mr. Foster, just finish filling out your statement and we'll talk later," Val said trying to ease the discomfort he was feeling. "Detective Morris, can you show me the scene?" She asked trying to direct the men away from each other.

He led Valerie to the small fence gate blocking the path that had recently been unlocked by a Florida Wildlife officer. Just then a breeze, that had been nonexistent all morning, chose now to stir up bringing with it the smell of death. She quickly covered her nose with her hand.

"That's not our vic if that's what you're thinking. This is the dumping site for the key deer that get struck and killed on the highway." Detective Morris reassured her.

"That is putrid!" she grimaced.

"After we go about 50 more yards, the smell will be behind us, unless the wind shifts."

"I hope so because I left my vapor rub in the car," She replied, referring to the practice of rubbing vapor rub under the nose to cut out the smell of decomposition.

A couple of minutes later she spotted Delaney bending over what was obviously another female victim with a crime scene photographer taking pictures from various angles. She stood back for a couple minutes to allow the photographer to finish his job.

Delaney looked up at Valerie and gave her a look of sadness mixed with compassion. She said nothing as Valerie walked up and took her first look at the second girl.

As she grew closer, she could tell this young woman looked nothing like the first. This young woman was a light skinned African American with a light sprinkle of freckles across her nose. Her hair was very short and was probably stylish in life, but now was just a soaked mess from the couple inches of water and mud she was lying in. She lay face up in muddy water and her eyes, uninhabited by life, stared sightless up into the sky.

"It looks like the same COD as the last girl but of course, I'll let you know for certain when the autopsy is complete," Delaney finally spoke breaking the silence.

"What is going on here?" Val said more to herself than anyone else. "This place is usually so peaceful."

"I agree. It has to be someone that is familiar to the area with them being dumped so close together," Detective Morris chimed in.

"Or, someone is extremely clever and knows the island is fairly quiet and the path of least resistance when it comes to getting rid of bodies," Val suggested canceling out his theory.

"I have lived here my entire life, and we have had missing people who have never been found, and some that have been found after the bones have been bleached out by the sun, but you and I both know this is entirely different. I guess I have always taken the peace here for granted."

She felt a little sorry for him. It was hard for her to muster up the energy for this job sometimes, and at his age, it must be getting harder with each passing day.

"It's very disturbing, but we'll get it figured out. If it turns out that we think we have, and God help me for saying this, a serial killer, we will have to call the FBI. Let's wait and see what the ME comes up with."

Detective Morris' phone rang. He answered and walked away from Valerie and Delaney.

"Can you send someone back now to help me get her bagged and loaded?" Delaney asked. Before Val had a chance to go ask someone, Detective Morris returned.

"You are not going to believe this, but Marine Patrol just found another body on the back side of Cudjoe Island. It's accessible, but the shoreline has some sharp rocks along it. It might not be related. It could just be someone who drowned, but I think it's worth looking into. You'll be getting the body anyway." He said directing that to Delaney.

"I'll certainly look for any similarities." Delaney assured him.

"Well, let's hope it has nothing to do with this," Val despaired. She said her goodbyes to Delaney and Detective Morris and told him she would see him back at the substation. She made her way back down the trail and over to Al Foster who still waited a little ways from the entrance.

"Mr. Foster, it's time you and I had a long talk."

Chapter 8

Valerie made her second stop of the day at the Sheriff's substation to talk with Detective Morris. She knew he would have plenty of questions pertaining to her interview with Al Foster.

Even though he was the only person who could reasonably be a suspect at his point, her gut instincts told her to look elsewhere. She knew this would cause friction with Morris.

She started down the hall towards his office and saw he had someone in there already talking with the door closed. Not wanting to interrupt, she decided to go get a cup of coffee up front while she waited for him to finish. Turning around suddenly, she ran in to a broad, muscular chest. She looked up into the most unusually colored eyes she had ever seen. They were a gunmetal gray/blue mix. She could get lost in them, and did for several seconds until her common sense returned. She got an odd feeling she had seen him before, but swore she would have remembered someone who looked like him.

"Sorry," she apologized with a voice that seemed small.

"It's okay. It happens," the man looked amused.

"Yeah ... well ... sorry." Val said again clearing her throat. God, I am an idiot she thought. Her mouth was suddenly dry and her heart was beating a little faster than normal.

"No harm done." He replied in a deep but quiet voice. He was making no attempt to move, but suddenly dropped his gaze to her hand on his chest, where she had tried to steady herself after bumping onto him.

Embarrassed beyond belief, she quickly dropped it like she had been burnt. She smiled and said, "I need to go that way," pointing towards the front.

"Yeah, sure." He stepped to the side allowing her to pass.

She could feel his eyes on her as she walked away and it made her whole body tingle. He was incredibly handsome. She could not believe the way she had reacted to him. It wasn't like her at all. She felt as if she were in high school all over again and had just had a run in with the popular high school quarterback. It had been a long time since she had felt that strong of an attraction to any man, and was not sure how to feel about it. Her last boyfriend had been such an ass about her being a cop. He made her feel miserable and she had actually started doubting herself. Good thing she had caught him cheating and dumped his butt before he could do any more damage. She realized now that he was the one with all the insecurities. She smiled realizing she would finally have something exciting to share with Delaney when she saw her this afternoon. Delaney had much more experience dating and seemed to have most of the answers to Val's questions, though Val rarely took her advice, even after asking for it.

Reaching the front she glanced back quickly, but he had already vanished into one of the offices down the hall.

Instead of coffee, she decided some cold water would be better for her dry mouth, so she made her way over to the cooler. She had downed one cup and was halfway through her second when she saw Detective Morris walking his visitor out. She made her way over to them and Detective Morris noticing her, made introductions.

"Valerie, I would like you to meet Pastor Donald Lockhart. He is the pastor of the church my wife and I attend. He just returned from a conference. Pastor, this is Detective Valerie Mason. She is helping us out with the murder case on the island." She studied him closely and couldn't believe he could be wearing a three-piece suite in this weather. The pastor extended his hand to Valerie and greeted her with a huge smile, although it didn't quite reach his eyes. "Nice to meet you detective."

"Thank you, it's nice to meet you too," Valerie replied.

"The pastor came by to see if there was any news on the murder and ask if maybe there was any way he could help out by speaking to people and calming their fears." Detective Morris sounded appreciative of citizens that were willing to help.

"We don't have a lot to go on, but if anybody that attends your services has any information, we would appreciate you encouraging them to come forward. No matter how small it is, it could be helpful."

The preacher stared at Valerie for a few seconds and then nodded his head at her. "Guess it's time to get going. I hope to see you at church on Sunday, David, and that invitation is open to you too young lady." She hated when men used the term young lady. It sounded so condescending.

"My wife and I will be there." Detective Morris and Valerie watched him walk away. He stopped by the receptionist's desk and handed her a pamphlet out of his pocket. Morris glanced at Valerie sideways and said "You are welcome to join us on Sunday."

"Maybe another time. No offense, but he reminds me of one of those TV evangelists."

"He's one of the nicest guys I know." Morris defended.

"Ok. Well, I came by to fill you in on my interview with Al Foster."

"Did you get much from him?"

"Actually I did. I still don't believe he's our guy. He has just been unfortunate enough to be in the wrong place at the wrong time ... twice. After speaking with him, I found out he took pictures of the crowd at both crime scenes. The other day I asked him to send the one from the first one to me, because if our perp returned to the scene to watch the ensuing chaos he caused, he might be in the pictures."

"I know you don't like him for this, but right now he is all we have. I have background checks that have come in. He doesn't have a criminal record, but because he was a teacher his fingerprints are in the system, so we can compare them to any we find on the scenes."

"Well speaking of that, I am headed over to Marathon to the Coroner's office and find out what, if any, similarities the two cases have."

"Ok. I should let you know before you go that the FBI has gotten wind of this and might be sending someone here this afternoon, depending on what we find out from the coroner's report."

Valerie sighed," So be it, I just don't like them taking over when I am working on something. I know they have better resources and a lot more of them though, so that could be helpful."

"It'll be fine. I know how you feel, but I would like to see this thing wrapped up before I retire."

Valerie was aggravated. The thought of the FBI coming was enough to put her in a sour mood, but add to it Detective Morris focusing on his retirement instead of this case and she was ready to scream. She sighed inwardly and took a deep breath. Man, did she ever need night out.

She was even starting to look forward to it. She said her goodbyes to the detective and made her way past the receptionist's desk. As she passed by, she glanced down at the leaflet the preacher had left. It triggered something in the back of her mind, but what exactly, she couldn't put her finger on. She had probably found one stuck under her wiper blade in a parking lot at one time. She pushed it out of her thoughts and concentrated instead on the rest of the day ahead. She had quite a few things she needed to accomplish before quitting time, starting with a trip to Marathon.

~ ~ ~

Reed's pulse was off the charts, and he didn't think it would come down anytime soon. He stood by the window in Sheriff Jackson's office. The sheriff was only at the substation one day a week. The rest of the time he was at the main headquarters, and the other substations that he divided his time at. Since he was here today, Reed was called in to give his statement on the body he and Rick had found yesterday.

The sheriff was on the phone, so Reed was using the opportunity to check out the woman he had ran into in the hall earlier. She was the same one he had spotted from the patrol boat the other day as she watered flowers on the porch of a houseboat, now here she was at the sheriff substation. She was even more beautiful up close. For a moment he had been embarrassed thinking she had recognized him.

He could still feel her hand on his chest where she had placed it to steady herself from falling. He placed his hand over that spot unconsciously while watching her talk to two older men. One he knew was a detective, the other he had never seen before. He wondered what she was doing here, but the gun and badge she was wearing on her hips was a good

85

indicator that she was a deputy too. Most likely a detective, since she was not wearing a standard uniform.

The sound of the sheriff hanging up the phone startled him out of his thoughts. He turned around and the sheriff indicated for him to have a seat. He then questioned Reed as to the events that occurred leading up to the discovery of the body on the shoreline of Cudjoe. He gave the sheriff a verbal statement and then a copy of his written report. He also included a copy of the report they had taken from the group of fishermen the other day, just in case it somehow it all tied in together. The sheriff thanked him and told him he would be in touch if anything else came up.

Reed left the Sheriff's office and was walking back down the hall when he passed the open door to the detective's office he had seen speaking to the woman he had bumped into. He knocked lightly to get the man's attention.

Detective Morris looked up. "Something I can help you with son?"

"Yes, sir, I was wondering if the young lady with the dark hair you were speaking with earlier works here."

"You must mean Valerie. She is a MCSO detective working on the murder case here."

"Thank you. I appreciate your help." And with that he walked away and wondered why he had never met her before today.

"Do you now?" Detective Morris said and leaned back in his chair with a big all-knowing grin on his face.

Chapter 9

For the second time this week, Valerie parked and walked up to the front door of the Coroner's office. This time though she walked right in. Today the staff had arrived, so no need for Delaney to buzz her in. She stopped at the front desk to show her ID and sign in, and then made her way to the autopsy room. Delaney was at her desk working when Val walked in. She never even looked up.

"I'm still working on the reports for the second one. I am not ready for the third yet," she called out.

"I am just here for the second one."

"Oh, it's you. I thought it was Eric coming back down to prepare for our next exam."

"I just came by to see what you had so far, if anything."

"It looks like the same person killed both girls. The marks around the throats are identical in size and pattern. Neither one was sexually assaulted, but the most telling sign is they both have needle marks above the elbows indicating that they were drugged. I won't know by what though until toxicology reports are back. That could take several weeks."

"Too bad it doesn't work as fast as it does on TV."

"Wouldn't that be a hoot?" Delaney said smiling. "I still have to do the autopsy of the third girl, but I won't get to her until after lunch. I'll let you know something as soon as I know. She has been in the water, so that one will be messy." Val screwed her face up. She didn't know how Delaney did this job sometimes. It was bad enough seeing the body in the shape she found them in, but to actually do the autopsies ... she shuddered. Wanting to clear her mind of those images she said, "I have been thinking about tomorrow night."

"Oh no you don't! You are not backing out on me!"

"Relax, I am not backing out on you, I am actually looking forward to it after the week I've had."

"It has been a pretty rough one for everyone. I have never had this many autopsies in a span of three days. I have the three girls that were found plus an old man who died in his sleep at home and was found by a neighbor."

"Well I for one will be glad to sip on a margarita and listen to some reggae," Valerie said with an odd grin on her face.

Delaney narrowed her eyes suspiciously. "Spill it. What's going on?"

"Nothing. Why?"

"Nothing? You are looking forward to going out to have a margarita and listen to some reggae? Something has you in a weird mood, weird for you anyway."

"I ran into someone today. Literally. He was ... nice," she said with a small giggle.

Delaney couldn't help but smile. "Nice, huh? Nice as in he's a gentleman or nice as in nice butt?"

"I didn't get a look at his butt, but if it looks like the rest of him I am sure it is, and we barely spoke, but he was gorgeous."

Delaney couldn't help herself. She laughed again, "Oh my God, I have never seen you like this. You're acting like a normal person." Valerie blushed.

"Well do me a favor, and help me find out who he is. He had a marine patrol emblem on his shirt. I know Rick is in that unit, so maybe he knows him."

"I'll see what I can do, but telling Rick he is nice or gorgeous isn't much of a description for him to go on. You can describe him tomorrow night to see if he knows who he is.

"Ok. So what time are we meeting and where?"

"Seven thirty at The Palms Patio."

"I'll be there."

"Maybe I'll even get you up there to do karaoke."

"Delaney, don't push it. It's enough I agreed to go out, but there is not enough alcohol in Key West to get me to go up on a stage to sing," Val said wagging her finger at her.

"The way I look at it, you caved on one thing, so maybe you will on the other."

"Not likely."

"Ok, I give up. For now. See you tomorrow night. I'll send you those reports as soon as I can."

"Oh, just to give you a heads up, you might have the FBI wanting all your reports too."

"Gee, thanks."

"Anything for a friend." Val walked out waving. She was feeling good despite the week so far. She had high hopes that Delaney would find some conclusive evidence from both girls that would give them a clue to the killer's identity.

She was going to stop by the second scene to see if she could get a feel for the whole thing. Sometimes walking through a scene after everyone had left, was more helpful to her than when everyone was traipsing around it.

On the road again, she thought as she pulled out on US1 headed back towards Big Pine. The drive was uneventful which gave her time to think. She turned her air conditioner up a couple of notches. Why did it have to be so damn muggy when she had work to do outside? Sometimes she thought she should have listened to her dad and become a teacher. On second thought, she could tolerate the heat a lot better than she could tolerate being in a classroom with twenty plus kids all day. She liked kids well enough, just not enough to tolerate a classroom full of them for eight hours.

Her dad hated her choice of occupation, which is probably what drove her harder to become a LEO. He had certainly made enough of his own bad decisions that she was not exactly ready to follow his advice. Besides, she needed to make her own decisions, even if they turned out not to be the right ones. So far, she thought, I have done pretty well for myself.

As if her dad coming down on her for her job wasn't enough, she had the misfortune to date a guy a lot like her dad in the fact he didn't like her career. He said it was too dangerous for her. Val always figured it made him feel emasculated that she was a deputy and he was a chef. Too damn bad. She didn't choose his career for him, and no one was going to choose hers or tell her what she should and shouldn't do. If a man had problem with that, it was his problem, not hers.

Arriving at the second crime scene, she could see that it was still cordoned off by yellow tape. There was also an officer sitting in a car. After speaking to him and showing her ID, she realized he was patrolling between the two scenes to keep an eye on everything until they were reopened to the public. He told her there had been no one around ether spot. She thanked him and headed down the nature trial.

The gravel made a crunching sound under her feet. It was the only sound that could be heard out here in the morning stillness. The heat was probably keeping all the wildlife hidden under trees and bushes for shade until the late afternoon/early evening when they would come out to eat and drink in the cooler part of the day. The hike, if one was not traveling the path to the scene of a murder, was quite beautiful.

Palmettos lined the trail and there were plenty of Blackbeard and Cats Claw bushes. She was surrounded by a sea of green and brown. Every now and then she would see a pop of color from a wild flower. She always wondered how botanists came up with names for flowers as strange as they were.

The pine trees were tall and majestic with their tops pointing straight into the sky. Often, the trees were the unfortunate target of lightening, and there were several fallen over, that had met this fateful end. Some were still standing, but marred by burn marks. Usually, you could hear the wind whispering through their tops, but not today. The silence was eerie.

She suddenly had a strange thought.

I am not alone.

Stop being ridiculous Valerie. Why would anyone be out here unless they had to be as hot as it is right now? She stopped mid path to look around and listen. No sounds, not even birds chirping. A couple of zebra butterflies flew out on the path in front of her. The only sign of life she had seen so far.

The trail was winding, and it took about ten minutes to reach the second scene. She compared both of them and there was nothing to indicate that the murders had occurred at either location. The only spot at scene one was where the grass had been flattened by the body that had been placed there, and here the body was found in a small marsh area that had approximately two to three inches of transparent brown colored water. It resembled soda that had sat for so long the ice had melted in it and watered it down. The grass was trampled down now, but she would bet that was from the crime scene techs after the body had been removed. This set of crime scene pictures would need to be gone over very closely when she got back to her office, especially shoe imprints in the mud. They might be able to determine shoe size and what type of shoe it was.

She had to face it, there was not a solitary clue that she could see here. Just like the other scene. Hot and frustrated she felt like screaming, instead she let a huge sight that blew the bangs up and off her forehead.

She made her way back to her truck and drove down Key Deer Boulevard towards the end of the island, where it was all residential, to get a good idea of the lay of the land. For a mile or so the scenery was the same, just pine forest on either side of the road. It was the only pine barren left in the Keys and it was protected.

Every now and then the thick pines would open up and you would see a building. So far she had seen a fire station, a minimum security prison facility, a baseball field and a couple of churches. As she passed by one church, The Church of the Islands, she noticed the sign out front announcing Sunday service at eleven a.m. Looking at that sign, there was a bell that dinged somewhere in the back of her mind just like it did back at the station when she had seen the pamphlet that Reverend Lockhart had given the receptionist.

What was so familiar about it? It was just a basic pamphlet and as far as that goes, so was the church sign. She wasn't sure, but she also knew her mind worked in strange ways sometimes when she was trying to piece together a case. I just have to let it do its thing she thought, it hasn't let me down so far.

She pulled over in the church parking lot intending to turn around, but decided to park. She was just about to get out to look around when she noticed a man coming out the front door. It was the same man she had met the other day when she had lunch with Detective Morris. He turned and went around the side of the building. A few moments later he pulled out in a dark colored sedan. She decided to follow him and trailed just far enough behind him that she would appear to be just another vehicle on the road. She noticed he slowed down to a rolling stop as he came close to the Jack Watson trail and then again at the Blue Hole. Was it out of curiosity like so many others, or something else? She pulled up behind him at the intersection to read his tag number.

1PRCHR.

Seriously, a pastor had a vanity plate and it was number one preacher? This was an example of everything that was wrong with this world.

He had seemed odd to her the other day, and now he really piqued her interest. She just might have a new suspect. He looked the part too, just plain creepy. She knew you couldn't suspect people based on looks because it had nothing to do with it. There were plenty of examples throughout history of nice looking people committing heinous crimes. Actions did speak volumes though, and he was acting a bit suspicious. He turned towards Key West. What good luck she thought, so am I. She followed him all the way into Key West. He turned into a well-known shelter for women that was run by a collaboration of churches. She watched for a few minutes as he was greeted by a young lady with a hug then opened the door for him as carried in a couple of boxes. He was most likely there on church business and there is nothing suspicious about that.

So why then did she have a nagging feeling about him?

Chapter 10

After a brief stop at Cudjoe Key substation to see a couple of buddies, Reed drove along the highway south to Key West. The site of the cerulean water never got old no matter how many times he saw it. It was breathtaking to the tourists who had never experienced it before, and was to him too, even though he had lived here most of his life and saw it every day. He rolled the windows down to breathe in the briny ocean air. It had a calming effect when he inhaled it deeply.

His thoughts drifted back to finding the dead woman yesterday. What a tragic end. In life, he was sure she had been pretty, but the sea life along that shoreline had made her into a small feast. It was bad, but he had seen worse so he didn't think she had been there long. There were some small areas on that shore where people hung out and partied, and he wondered if she fell victim to one of them, or maybe it had been an accident and she had been too drunk or high to save herself. The CSI and coroner unit had shown up soon after the discovery and took over, so he and Rick backed off and let them do their thing. Now he had to wonder if that group of fishermen from the other day had been right about seeing a body, even though it was found a few miles from where they had spotted something. He and Rick had been told to write their reports and show up this morning to give a verbal statement to the Sherriff so if he had any questions they could be answered directly. Rick was giving his statement tomorrow because he had another appointment this morning.

Looking out across the water as he crossed one of the last bridges before reaching Key West, he thought about how nice it would be out there on his own personal boat. It would be even nicer with the beautiful Detective at his side. He could not get her out of his head.

"Valerie," he said aloud. He loved the way it rolled off his tongue.

He planned on asking around the station to see if anyone knew her. Of course he did have the patrol boat docked close to her houseboat, so it was almost certain that he would see her again. As he passed by Garrison Bight Marina, he looked over at the row of rainbow colored houseboats and smiled.

It had been about 9 months since he had dated anyone and he had never gone that long without the company of a woman. That made him sound like an ass, but he knew he wasn't. He always treated any woman he dated with the utmost respect, and always made sure her wants and needs came first. He needed to change his direction of thought. He had not even met her and he was already planning what he would do if he got her alone.

Rick had invited him out to dinner tomorrow night, and a few beers seemed to be just what he needed. Friday could not get here fast enough.

~ ~ ~

Val's cell rang but she couldn't reach it. Her purse was in the back and she hadn't thought to grab it before she started down the road. If it was important they would call back. A few seconds after it stopped, it rang again. She found a small pull off on the side of the road and reached back to get her purse. Before she could get, it stopped ringing again. She looked at the caller ID and did not recognize the number, even though it was a local one. She was about to put it in the cup holder of the console when it rang again.

"Hello" she answered.

"Val ... I need ... where are ... me."

"Brianna? You're breaking up."

"Can't ... long ... Call ... name ...Tony."

"Call who? What have you gotten into?" Val was met by silence. "Bri?"

Static, then "scared ... soon, please." The line went dead.

Just freaking great! Give me just enough to worry, but not enough to help. She immediately tried to dial her sister back but saw that the caller ID listed the number as unknown and therefore could not be called back. Damn!

She dialed her dad's number instead, and when he answered, she asked if he had heard from Brianna lately.

"Not in a couple of months," he sighed.

"She just called. I couldn't understand much because the line was breaking up. She sounded as if she was in some kind of trouble."

"You shouldn't worry. I bet she's fine. Just trying to get you all upset so you'll feel bad and give her money, or a place to stay,"

"I hope that's all it is. She sounded, I don't know, different this time."

"I'm sure that's all it is."

Not really satisfied but not wanting to argue or stress her father. She changed the subject. "How have you been Dad?"

"Ok, I guess. The diabetes got out of whack but it's doing better now. Would be a lot better if you came for a visit every once in a while"

"Why didn't you call if you were sick? I have been really busy, but I would have taken some time off to come up and check on you."

"You have your own life that doesn't include taking care of your old man." He sounded a bit deflated and older than he was, making her feel guilty.

"I'll get some time off this summer and come home for a couple of weeks."

"Ok, I'm going to hold you to it."

"Yes, sir, I know you will. Love you daddy."

"I love you too, honey. Bye."

"Bye."

Great. Now she was worried about her sister and feeling guilty about her father. Could she ever just have a normal life? She supposed not. To have a normal life, you must have a normal family, and her family was way outside the boundaries of normal. Still, as worried as she was, she couldn't help being a little aggravated. Why couldn't Brianna just grow the hell up and be a productive member of society? She had mentioned the name Tony. He was probably her latest boyfriend. She sighed inwardly, Friday night was around the corner. She planned to use it to let go of all the stressors that this week had chosen to dump at her feet.

A couple of hours later, just as she was getting ready to leave work, the phone on her desk rang. It was Delany with the news that the third girl found had no signs of being killed like the other two. She told Valerie that this case was simple. The girl apparently had been high and most likely went for a swim, based on the fact she had been in a bikini, and had drowned because her senses and reactions were possibly dulled by the drugs found in her system. They would know soon enough when the tox screen came in.

Even though that was a horrible way to die, Val was just glad they did not have a third murder victim on their hands. She hoped it would stay that way too, even though she wasn't holding her breath.

Chapter 11

Val found herself feeling excited. It was finally Friday. It was unfamiliar for her to be looking forward to something she normally would not give a second thought. She changed clothes at least four times before settling on the right outfit. Why? She asked herself. It's not a date, just dinner with friends.

She finally decided on a sundress with spaghetti straps. It was cool and airy, just perfect for warm Florida nights. The top layer was an aqua blue, sheer material and the under dress was royal blue soft cotton. When the two colors swirled together it reminded her of the ocean waves moving toward shore. The two fabrics and colors were beautifully matched.

The one thing about Valerie that would probably surprise most people is that she loved feminine clothes and makeup. Her job required the most unflattering look, so in her free time she loved to indulge her girly side.

She pulled a pair of silver strapped sandals out of the closet to finish off the look. With her hair freshly blow-dried and just the right amount of make-up applied, she was ready. She jogged down the stairs and made sure all the lights were off, except the one over the stove and the small lamp right by the door. Those two were always left on if she would be coming in after dark. She dropped her cell in her purse after turning it to vibrate. She needed it with her for emergencies but did not want any unnecessary interruptions ruining her evening.

Walking out the door and locking it, she headed down the dock that served as a sidewalk of sorts in between the rows of houseboats. Making her way through the parking lot, she found her powder blue '67 Mustang. It had been a graduation gift from her father when she finished high school. He restored it himself, claiming it gave him something to do to keep his mind off drinking when he was trying to quit. He had never been a drinker ironically until her mother died, after he claimed alcohol had caused all their marital problems, and eventually her death.

Stop it Valerie! You are not going there tonight. Damn, even the simplest of things could somehow ruin her good mood. But not tonight, she wouldn't let it. She was ready to relax a little and have some fun.

She made her way downtown to Duval Street. It was the most famous street in Key West and was home to such popular places like Sloppy Joes where Hemingway had loved to hang out.

Already teeming with people out on the town, she maneuvered very carefully along the street filled with pedestrians, mopeds, and pedicabs. She finally arrived at The Palms Patio and pulled around to park in the back. There were not many parking spaces but she had arrived early enough to get one. She noticed that Delaney's Miata was there already. She rolled her window down and received a hangtag parking pass from the parking attendant for her rearview mirror. She hung it, then checked her hair and makeup one last time. She stepped out of the car and straightened her dress. She walked around the side of the restaurant that was an open aired eating area, and made her way to the greeter at the door. She informed him that she was meeting friends who were already here and looked around. She caught sight of Delaney and Rick sitting at a table facing her. They both waved her over. She quickly walked over and after hugging both of them she took a seat across from Delaney.

"I'm so glad you decided to come", Delaney almost squealed with delight.

"Me too. I need this."

The waitress arrived to take her drink order. She had decided before she got here it would be a Margarita.

"Ok, right to the good stuff. Now, describe this dreamy stud muffin to Rick."

Val's face deepened a few shades of red. Rick chimed in with a laugh "Wow, he must be something to have you looking like you're sunburned."

"Shut up, both of you," she said with an added grin.

"Spill it, what does this dude look like?"

"Well he was tall, probably about six one or two, very muscular build. Dark blonde hair with a crew cut. Stunning blue-gray eyes and a strong chin with a dimple."

"If I didn't know better, I would swear you were describing Reed, but then again, I think he's ugly as hell."

"Who exactly is Reed?"

"He happens to be my partner and standing right behind you."

No, it can't be. Valerie thought. What if he had heard her description of him? Delaney and Rick were both doing a good imitation of the Cheshire cat and Valerie knew without looking it was going to be him. She slowly turned and it was him. Damn, what would she do or say now? It was little consolation, but he looked just as surprised as she did.

"Valerie Mason, I would like you to meet my partner, and the mystery man in question judging from the looks on both of your faces, Reed Stone." Rick introduced them.

"Nice to meet you, again I mean." Reed stumbled a little with his words. He took her extended hand to shake it and found himself not wanting to let it go. He noticed she wasn't pulling away either.

"Nice to meet you too. Again," she responded shyly, but with a smile. After what seemed like an eternity, they let go of each other's hands. While the waitress had walked over to take his order, she had a chance to get Delaney's attention. She wanted to choke her. She had to have known exactly who she was talking about and invited him tonight. She gave her that you-and-I-will-talk-about-this-later look. Delaney mouthed back silently that she swore she hadn't known.

"So you two have met already?" Rick asked sarcastically.

"We met yesterday in Big Pine" they said at the same time. Everyone laughed, and it seemed to break the ice.

"By the way Rick, what do you mean you think I am ugly as hell?" Reed pretended he was offended.

"You are."

"You aren't winning any beauty contests either."

"Boys please, you're both gorgeous and you know it, which I would suspect is the real problem. You each think you're better looking than the other."

"I am better looking. At least I hope you think so." Rick tickled Delaney in the ribs.

One of Jimmy Buffett's slower songs started playing so Rick asked Delany to dance. He winked at Reed as if to say, no need to thank me for giving you a few minutes alone with her.

"So, you're working on the double murders on Big Key?" Reed asked trying to make small talk and feeling like an ass for asking an obvious question.

"Yes. Delaney told me today that the third girl found was an accidental drowning. I know now it was you and Rick that found her. I thought he might know who you were when we met at the substation, but never figured on you being his partner."

"Guess it's a small world."

"A small island you mean."

"That too." He smiled the most disarming smile she had ever seen. Even his teeth were perfect.

She realized she was going to have to be very careful around this one. He was the type of guy that would be way too easy to fall for. Then again, why shouldn't she let herself fall? Where had that thought come from? Her emotions were all over the place, or should she say her hormones?

"Care to dance," he asked.

"I'm really not that good." She blushed.

"Me either. Maybe one day, we can learn to dance together." The implication of that statement, intended or not, caused butterflies in her stomach. Delaney and Rick soon rejoined them at the table and said they were ready to order. The dancing had made them realize how hungry they were.

"I'm starving too," Reed said casting a sideways glance, and winking at Valerie, causing her to blush again. She wasn't used to so much flirtation.

The waitress took their orders and brought another round of drinks, except for Val because she had to drive home later and that first one had been pretty strong. She never even thought about that or she would have called a cab. It just showed her lack of experience at going out on the town. They all enjoyed the ambience of the place and the next couple of hours drifted by as they discussed everything from the cases they were working on, to meeting next Saturday to go out boating to Picnic Island together. None of them were scheduled to work, which was almost like a small miracle, or maybe fate.

Delany and Rick decided they were going to call it a night, and after paying for Val's dinner as she had promised, even though Valerie protested, Delany gave Val a quick hug goodnight. She and Rick walked out hand in hand.

"They make a cute couple. Do you think the two of them might get married one day?" Val asked.

"I know Rick talks about having a big family, so I guess anything's possible."

"Delaney is an only child, so I am not sure how she'll feel about a bunch of kids, then again she might be open to it."

"How about you?" he asked putting her on the spot.

"I ... uh ... haven't given it much thought. I don't have a big family. I have one sister, my mom's dead, and my dad lives in Clewiston. It's a small town on Lake Okeechobee."

"I've heard about it from my fishing buddies. I have a bother that lives in Ft. Lauderdale. My parents live here and own a restaurant right off of Duval Street."

"Really? Why didn't we eat there tonight?"

"I eat there plenty. It's nice to go somewhere else for a change."

"I will have to check it out for lunch one day."

"You'll love it. The food is great because my mom is an awesome cook. It's called Stone's Bistro Garden. You can sit inside, or dine outside in a beautiful garden that has 3 different water fountains."

"It sounds beautiful and romantic." She said, and for some reason, that caused him to smile.

He stared at her for several moments and then broke the trance by looking at his watch. "As much as

Angela Jarvis

I would love to sit here with you all night, I have to work in the morning. It's almost midnight."

"I understand. I didn't realize it was so late or I wouldn't have kept you," Val apologized.

"Don't apologize, I can think of no other way I would like to be kept," he said smiling that charming smile again. She must be getting used to his flirting, she didn't even blush that time. "Can I walk you to your car?"

"Sure. I'm around back. Are you?"

"I live on Angela Street, so I walked."

"Would you like me to drop you off?"

"Not that I couldn't use the exercise, but any excuse to be with you a while longer is a good one."
"Just what I was thinking." Did she say that out loud? Where had that come from? The two of them laughed, only now it felt more comfortable to her, instead of awkward, but she could still feel the butterflies in her stomach.

The drive to Angela Street was only a few blocks and they made small talk, learning more little things about each other along the way. Following his directions, she pulled up in front of a charming Key West Cottage. It was white with blue shutters from what she could see in the headlights pointing towards the house. "It's adorable," she said in awe.

"Adorable? Just what every guy wants to hear, but I did inherit it after my grandparents died, and they were an adorable couple."

"I'd love to see it in the daylight."

"You're welcome here anytime."

"I'm sorry, that was rude. I didn't mean to invite myself over."

"Like I said, you're welcome here anytime. No need to ask. Thanks for the ride."

"No problem at all."

107

"I had a good time tonight and really enjoyed meeting you. Maybe we can do it again soon. Just the two of us," he added hopefully.

"I would love that."

He paused a moment then said, "I have a confession to make. I have seen you once before we met at the substation. You were on the porch of your houseboat watering your plants."

She didn't know how to respond. That's where she had recognized him from! She had caught him staring at her while she had been dressed in nothing but a robe. He was a guy after all. "I live on the houseboat. I see Marine Patrols boats coming and going all the time but I just never really paid that close attention. I thought you seemed familiar when we ran into each other." She did not elaborate further.

Not knowing what else he could say to keep from having to get out, he opened the door and stepped out. He bent down looking through the opened window and told her bye. She responded the same. She waited until he unlocked the door and then backed out. He turned and waved as he closed the door.

She felt herself feeling utter disappointment that he had not even tried to kiss her goodnight. What the hell is wrong with you Valerie, she thought, you hardly know the guy? Oh, but she wanted to get to know him *a lot* better. This has been a night full of surprises, she thought. She was surprised to find out he was Rick's friend, but she found herself being most surprised at her reaction to him. She felt as if she was on a roller coaster and it was steadily making its way to the top. How long would it take to get there, and go free falling down the other side?

~ ~ ~

Reed let out a big sigh as he closed the front door. It had taken every ounce of the gentleman his mother had pounded into him, not to pull Valerie into his arms tonight and kiss her senseless. He got the vibe she would have been agreeable. The dress she had on was enough to drive any man crazy, and it matched her eyes perfectly. He had felt foolish at times tonight making small talk, but he had to have a reason to look at her simply because he couldn't take his eyes off of her. He had never had a problem talking with women, hell most of them threw themselves at him and he didn't have to do much work at all. Valerie was different. She might be a bit of challenge but he could tell she was interested.

Chapter 12

The caseload had never been crazier than it was at the moment for Val since she moved here. MCSO was dealing with a shipwreck off the Southernmost Point that turned out to be hauling a cargo load of heroin. The crew was believed to be holed up here in town somewhere. They were using a lot of manpower to look for them and their known associates. To top that off, Spring Break was in full swing, the bars and hotels were overflowing, and Val had two murders on her hands.

The icing on the cake ... it was Monday. The weekend was never long enough. She needed a day in between Saturday and Sunday. When she moved here, it was to have a quieter life and an easier job. Working in Miami-Dade had become too hectic for her. She had seen a lot in her career there, and was amazed at the evil mankind could perpetrate upon his fellow man.

Today, she was meeting the boss of a young woman who had been reported missing by some coworkers in Marathon at the coroner's office at 10:30 a.m. Detective Morris had called to let her know they had someone that reported a coworker missing and that fit the description of the first girl they had found. Val might have a little more to go on if it turned out to be her. She was keeping her fingers crossed that this might be the break she needed.

She had also been informed that she had a meeting this afternoon with Special Agent Anthony Giovanni from the FBI. She hoped he was not the pushy type that liked to throw his weight around. Only time would tell.

She stopped in at Big Pine to tell Detective Morris where she was headed and asked if he could tag along. He did, so they headed to Marathon. Along the way, they speculated on the different aspects of the case. For some reason, she held back on her suspicions about Pastor Cross. She didn't really know how Detective Morris felt about him, but she knew he was good friends with Pastor Lockhart, and didn't want him saying anything unwittingly. They both agreed on the hope that today would bring some closure.

Arriving at the coroner's office, they waited in the lobby for Patrick Montgomery to arrive. He and Ali's coworkers were very anxious about her, according to Detective Morris' previous conversation with him. A man of about fifty-five walked through the door and told the receptionist who he was. Valerie overheard his introduction and knew this was the man they were waiting for. She walked over to him and introduced herself, as well as Detective Morris.

"We're the ones assigned to this case," she explained. They shook hands.

"I heard the description of the girl found on the news. When Ali didn't show up for work, we all got worried. She has never been late or called in sick. She is one of the most reliable workers I have."

"Does she have any next of kin or family here?"

"She's from Boston. Her parents don't even know she is missing, I didn't want to worry them unnecessarily until I knew for sure."

"I understand. Are you ready?" Val asked. She could see that he looked uneasy, so hoping to make him feel a little better she said "You'll be looking at her on a monitor, so there's no need to worry about seeing her in person." She knew not many people could handle seeing a lifeless body, and wanted to put his mind at ease, if there was such a thing, when identifying a person's remains.

"Sure, let's get it over with."

They walked the long hallway back to a room set up for just this purpose. Valerie had called ahead to let Delaney know to have everything ready. All they had to do now was ring the buzzer on the wall and turn on the monitor.

The room was quiet and still as the door closed, and all outside noise disappeared. Valerie walked over, rang the buzzer, and switched on the monitor. They watched as Delaney pulled the sheet down to the shoulders.

They heard Mr. Montgomery suck in his breath. "That's her. That's Ali." He said in a voice that was too small for a man of his size. He looked pale, so Valerie offered him a seat.

He refused. "I'm fine."

"I have to ask if you're positive on the ID."

"I'm positive. That hair..." He couldn't finish his sentence. Looking at the screen once more with eyes that brimmed with tears he asked, "What will I tell her parents?"

"We can take care of that for you, if you'd like"

"I think it would be better for me to do it. I met them when they were here on vacation. She was their only child."

"We're truly sorry, Mr. Montgomery, for you, your staff and her family." Detective Morris finally spoke. He had been quiet the entire time after telling Valerie earlier that he never knew what to say to people about these things, which had made his job difficult at times.

"Thank you, if there's nothing else you need from me, I think I'll be going."

"Go ahead. We know you're upset, so drive carefully."

"I'll be fine. Thanks for the concern."

They followed him out. "Poor fella looked devastated," Morris sighed, shaking his head. "It's gotta be hard when it's all on you to ID someone."

"Let's hope the other girl will be easy to ID as well. It might not tell us who the killer is, but maybe there is some connection between the two."

"That would make it easy, and I don't know about you Detective, but I am never that lucky."

"No harm in wishing."

They walked to the autopsy room. Valerie told Delaney that a positive ID had been made and that next of kin was being notified. She could release the body as soon as they arrived and signed all the proper paperwork.

"At least one family will have closure."

"Closure is overrated. Does anyone ever really have closure?" Valerie asked to no one in particular.

Delaney remained silent knowing Val's family history. Morris wasn't sure what she was talking about, so he just suggested that they be on their way back to Big Pine.

"If I get any of the tox reports in I'll send them to you," Delaney told them as she walked them out. "I still haven't received anything back."

"Thanks. I appreciate it."

Once in the car, Morris was quiet. Who knew what he was thinking, but Valerie was contemplating what she had said to Delaney. She had never felt as if she had received closure for her mom. Why? She knew exactly what happened that night. There was no mystery there. Her mom was driving after having a few drinks and lost control of the car in the rain killing herself, and injuring both Valerie and Brianna. Her sister worse than her. She had to stay in the hospital for 3 weeks after the accident, while Valerie went home that same night with her aunt and a broken arm, as well as a broken heart. Her dad had stayed at the hospital with Brianna. She would drive herself crazy trying to figure it out. She released an audible sigh.

Morris looked over at her. "Everything O.K.?"

"Yeah. This thing is never easy, no matter how many times you do it," she said referring to the body ID.

"I'm glad I can say I have not had to do it very often in my thirty years on the job."

"I've done it more times that I care to remember. It just comes with the job I guess."

"The hardest one for me was an accident involving a sixteen-year-old boy. His parents were friends of mine. They were good people, and the kid was great at baseball, had good grades, and wanted to go to med school. He was riding his bike home after school on a rainy day. A semi driver hit him and dragged him and his bike a half-mile before stopping, claiming he never saw him. A passing car flagged him down."

"That's awful."

"His parents and two older sisters were devastated. They all considered him the star of the family."

"It's never easy. The victim is always someone's family or friend, as I said the other day. I've had a couple of cases when no ID could be made. It's sad to think that at the end, there is no one there to claim you and give you a proper burial."

"Sometimes the way we live, determines the way we end up, with nobody there to care."

"I suppose." There was nothing else to say as far as she was concerned. For whatever reason, the case was getting under her skin and she didn't know why.

She did know that she was more determined than ever to figure this mess out and get this guy, she just hoped no one else had to die before she did.

~ ~ ~

The office air conditioning hummed softly in the background struggling hard to do its job and keep the heat at bay. Val was waiting for the agent from the FBI. Not sure what to expect put her nerves on edge. She was ready for any questions he might have, but not ready to turn the case over if it came to that.

She had her files and photos stacked on the table in the conference room where they would meet, then walked over to make a fresh pot of coffee. It was much too hot for her to drink a cup, but she had seen a lot of people who could drink it all day long. She was finishing up when she heard a quick knock and the door swung open.

Turning around she was met by Mr. Tall, Dark, and ruggedly handsome. He was very broad in the shoulders and had green eyes with an olive complexion. He looked more like a player in the NFL than an FBI agent.

"You must be Detective Mason. You fit her description anyway."

"Yes, but please, call me Valerie." Who in the world gave her description to this man?

"Anthony Giovanni. You can call me Tony. It's nice to meet you." They exchanged a handshake.

"Nice to meet you also. I made some coffee if you would like a cup" she motioned towards the pot.

"Don't mind if I do." He said walking towards the small table that held the coffee maker. He poured a cup, then turned and looked directly at her. "I guess I should start by saying that I am not here to take over this case. Quite frankly, you have two homicides that may or may not be related, but as of yet, there is not much evidence to support that. So with that being said, what we do have does not support the theory that we have a serial killer on our hands, although we can't rule it out." Swirling the coffee stirrer around in his cup, he took a seat at the table. "I am here to offer the variable resources that the FBI has, and I am willing to lend help any way I can. We know small departments can be limited by budget constraints as well as manpower."

Valerie was really confused. Why was he really here? This was not making much sense to her at all. He said himself it was too early to tell what they were dealing with. "Thank you. We appreciate any help we can get right now." Pointing to some of the photos on the table, she explained "We have a positive ID on the first girl. Her name is Alicia Musgrave. Ali to her friends and family. She was 24 years old, comes from a good family, who are currently in route to claim her and take her home. She worked at a local bar and grill as a waitress. Her boss is the one who ID'd her." She noticed a look of confusion on his face.

"And the second victim?" he asked scanning through the next set of crime scene pictures.

"We haven't been able to identify her yet. We are working on her fingerprints to see if anything turns up in CODIS. Hopefully we'll get a hit. So far, no descriptions of anyone missing from this area fits."

"Do you have any suspects?"

"There is the man who found both bodies, Al Foster. It's strange he found them both to say the least, and in remote locations, but I've interviewed him and he just doesn't fit the profile of any type of criminal, much less a serial killer. The only other..." She stopped herself. She had not wanted to tell him her suspicion about the pastor, but why?

"Yes?"

"It's just a hunch, nothing really," She said hoping he would drop it.

"That's the way we operate best right, on a hunch? Some of the most difficult cases have been solved on one."

She hesitated. "There's something off about this pastor at the church on Big Pine. The problem is I can't place him at either scene, and there is absolutely no reason to suspect him." She watched his face to see if she could read it and thought she saw recognition when she mentioned the pastor's name.

"I am a bit confused by the fact that he's a preacher and you're suspicious of him."

"Me too. Like I said, it's just a hunch. He's strange and ... I just don't know. I found out he helps run a shelter here in Key West for young troubled women. Not that it has anything to do with this, at least I don't think so. I just can't help but feel he is somehow connected, I just don't have anything to back me on that theory. It's frustrating."

"Well, we have to go on facts right now and we don't have many of these. Do you mind if I sit here and go over these photos?"

"Help yourself. Maybe you'll see something I didn't. I have a few phone calls to make and some paperwork. I'll check back in with you in a bit. If you need anything, just pop your head out."

"Thanks."

She sat down on her desk and looked towards the conference room. The blinds were open so she could see him sitting at the table studying the photos and staring intently at one of them in particular. The problem was she didn't know which picture he was studying so intently. He took his cell phone out of his pocket and made a call. Too bad she couldn't read lips, she'd know if he was calling someone about the case. Of course, it could be personal too. He stood up suddenly and walked towards the door.

Valerie acted like she was busy and had not just been sitting there spying on him. He came towards her desk. She looked up as he approached.

"I'm finished. Do you think I can get a copy of everything sent to my hotel? I am staying at The Golden Sands Resort."

"Courtesy of the tax payers of course," She said jokingly.

"Of course." He smiled.

"I'll see to it that they're delivered this afternoon."

"Thank you. Here's my card, if you need anything. Remember, you have all our resources at your disposal."

"I appreciate it." She accepted the card and glanced at it quickly.

"Just doing my job." He smiled at her warmly, almost as if he was an old friend. He was certainly unusual.

Why did everyone seem suspicious to her? She was losing it, that's why. Maybe the killer was Al Foster. Maybe Pastor Cross was just a creepy looking man of the cloth and not a murderer. Maybe Brianna was getting her life together. And maybe, just maybe she would win the lottery tonight. The chances were about the same for all of it.

Chapter 13

Saturday morning lifted her head. She was all blue skies with puffy cotton ball clouds, and her sunshine streamed down like golden strands of hair towards the earth. It was a perfect day to be out on the ocean. Reed could tell the water would be smooth as glass ... perfect. His cell rang and he saw the number was Rick's.

"Hey bud, you all set?"

"Man, I'm sorry, I can't. That tooth I went to the dentist for the other day is killing me. The meds are giving me an upset stomach. Delaney is playing nurse so we're going to take a rain check."

Reed felt as disappointed as Rick sounded. "Sorry you aren't feeling good man, but the ocean isn't going anywhere. We'll set another date."

"I just feel bad, we've talked about it all week."

"Shit happens." He said with a laugh, knowing Rick would catch his literal meaning, referring to the upset stomach.

"Ha ha, funny guy. Feel better man. Later," he said hanging up the phone. He looked up just as Valerie was walking down the dock towards him, and he could not help but burst out laughing at her.

"You look like a tourist with all that stuff." He pointed at her big wide brimmed straw hat, and a huge beach bag filled with God knows what.

"I came prepared. I was a Girl Scout when I was younger."

Still laughing, he said "Well, let me ask you, are you prepared to be alone with me today? Rick just called and he and Delaney canceled. He has a tooth ache that is making him sick."

Valerie felt instant disappointment at the thought of her friend not going today, but at the same time, she felt tendrils of excitement building that she would have a chance to be alone with Reed.

"I hope he'll be okay. Toothaches are miserable."

"He'll be fine. He went to the dentist and has a prescription, so he should be fine once the meds kick in. Guess it's just you and me then." He seemed happy to know she didn't mind the change in plans.

They loaded all their gear in his twenty-six foot open fisherman. There was a compartment below the center console where they stored all the towels and things they didn't want to get wet and Reed sat a cooler in front of the console that held their drinks and lunch courtesy of his parent's bistro.

She stood beside him as he backed the boat out of the slip. He had thought of a different place to take her now that Rick and Delaney wouldn't be joining them. This place could be a little more secluded, and he wanted to get to know her better. It could be crowded at times, but the time of year, he knew the exact spot that would be perfect for this first date, even if she didn't realize yet that this is what today was.

They traveled north east of Key West about fifteen miles and finally reached the north side of Snipes Key. Reed cut the engine. "Umm, this is not Picnic Island," Val stated the obvious.

"Good observation. You might make first mate by the afternoon," he said grinning. "It's Snipes Key, a little less traffic and filled with a few surprises." He could see her uncertainty at not recognizing her surroundings. "Don't worry, I don't bite, unless you want me too." He said with a devious grin.

"I am not worried, I have a gun," she teased back.

"I guess I better be on my best behavior then. I just thought this would give us an opportunity to get to know each other."

Val smiled genuinely, but the butterflies had returned, and they felt as if they were growing into pterodactyls. She suddenly felt things were moving really fast.

They had to anchor about twenty yards from shore but the water was only waist deep. They grabbed their gear and put it in a small inflatable raft and walked to the beach pulling the raft behind them. Once they reached the beach, they placed all their things down and decided to go snorkeling. They swam in the shallow waters for a while pointing out fish and shells to each other. It had been a long time since Valerie had the opportunity to relax at the beach. Soon, the swimming had them famished, so they headed back to shore. Reed kept an old quilt to put down on the beach and he spread it out while she was rummaging through the cooler.

"How long did you plan on keeping me here? There is enough food for an army," she asked surprised at the amount of food in the cooler.

"Remember there was supposed to be four of us originally, two of which are growing boys who are always hungry."

She reached in pulling out a couple of sandwiches wrapped in wax paper and tied with baker's string. Tucked in the string were blue and white-checkered napkins that had his parents' restaurant logo on it. Next was a plastic container that had salami, feta, and cherry tomatoes on wooden skewers. A bottle of white Moscato was found next, and four generous slices of key lime pie each in its own plastic container, complete with a fork, was at the bottom.

They made quick work of the appetizer and the sandwiches. Valerie didn't know why, but food always tasted better in the fresh air. Everything had been delicious, and she eyed that key lime pie, but didn't have room for it at the moment. She wasn't a big drinker, so the two glasses of wine she had with her lunch had her feeling tipsy. She stretched out on the blanket feeling drowsy. The sunshine, the swim, and the food combined with the wine had her feeling lazy.

Reed lay down on his stomach beside her, and propped himself up on his elbows. "I take it you enjoyed your lunch?"

"Yes, definitely. I am stuffed. You were right, you're mom's food is awesome."

"She'll be happy you think so. There's key lime pie for dessert."

"I can't hold it right now. Maybe later," she said rubbing her belly.

His eyes couldn't help but follow her hand to her stomach. He studied her carefully. Her long black hair was still damp from their swim, but had salty "beach hair" waves. Her face was smooth and perfectly proportioned, and her eyes matched the ocean today. Her body was well toned and trim.

She noticed him looking her up and down and it made her body tingle. Their eyes met. "What would you say if I asked if I could kiss you?" he asked in a husky voice, almost a whisper.

"Why would you ask first?" she inquired giggling.

"You did remind me earlier you had a gun," he teased. Damn that grin of his.

"I do, but I left it on the boat."

"What kind of detective leaves her gun behind?"

"The kind that doesn't think she'll need it, or doesn't have a place to carry it in her bikini."

They both laughed at the image of her trying to find a place to put it. "You haven't answered my question."

"I don't intend to."

"How am I supposed to know then?"

"Figure it out for yourself."

"Okay, if you insist." He leaned towards her and kissed her softly at first, then with more pressure. She was instantly responsive, so he deepened the kiss. He ran his tongue along her lips and she opened to him. She wrapped her arms around his neck and pulled him in closer, and the kiss seemed to last forever.

Reed was the first to come up for air. He knew that he had to stop now, or things might go further than she was ready for. He looked down at her face and her eyes were half closed and softly glazed with passion. That was a look he could never get tired of, and one that he was going to make sure he got to see plenty of. To cool the moment he said jokingly "That wasn't so bad now was it?"

"I guess not, I've had worse," she answered. She loved to see his smile when she teased him.

His laughter was deep and he bent to kiss her again "Bet you'll never have better."

Thank God she was lying down. If not, she would have needed him to hold her up because her knees would have been jelly after that statement. His kisses were light this time and she knew he was trying to keep his composure.

"I have a surprise for you," he pulled back slowly and he whispered in her ear.

"What is it?"

"If I tell you, it won't be a surprise." He stood up and took her hands to help her up. She followed him down a small trail to another part of the beach. There was a small clearing that had a sandbar at low tide.

There, hanging from a tree branch, someone had hung a homemade swing. You could literally swing out over the water that at the moment was only knee deep. She thought it was one of the coolest things she had ever seen. How had she lived here all this time and not known about this?

"Reed this is so beautiful," she said with her voice full of awe.

"It's one of the reasons that I wanted to bring you here today, that and the kissing thing." He loved teasing her. She blushed and ran towards the swing. He walked up behind her and gave her a gentle push. She squealed with delight like a child causing him to laugh.

Kicking her feet higher each time she swung forward, Val realized that this day is just what she needed. A relaxing day with a gorgeous man never hurt a girl, that's for sure. Thinking about those kisses earlier sent warmth all the way to her core. She wondered how far she would have let him go if he had not stopped it when he did. It had been two years since her breakup with "Dirk the jerk" as Delaney called him. His kisses had never set her on fire like Reed's had. In fact, no guy she had ever dated had that effect on her just from a kiss. Not that she had a lot of experience to compare him to. She had dated some in college but nothing serious. She had had a brief fling with one of her academy instructors, which she should have known was a mistake from the beginning. She had been young, vulnerable, and easy to impress. She found out later she wasn't the only girl he was messing with. As a matter of fact, he had a reputation for it. She was glad for the distraction that the swing brought her, but she could not help wonder if he was feeling the same thing.

"Having fun?" he asked.

"Yes, I love it," her voice was full of enthusiasm. He laughed and kept pushing her. After a couple more minutes she decided to slow down and stop. He caught the swing when she had slowed enough and helped her out.

"That was incredible! I am definitely coming back here."

"Not without me I hope, who would give you a push?"

"I'm sure I could find a volunteer," she said teasingly. She could have sworn she heard a low growl come from his throat as he grabbed her around the waist as she tried to walk past him. Suddenly he was serious.

"Oh, like who?"

"I was kidding, Reed. There is no one else interested I can assure you," she said stunned by his reaction.

"Sorry. I shouldn't have reacted like that. My last girlfriend … never mind."

"It's okay. You can't help it if you're jealous of all this," she giggled trying to lighten the mood.

"I would be if I thought there was competition. I would have to step up my game," he admitted surprising himself. "Well then you have nothing to worry about. There hasn't been anyone for two years."

"Nine months here. She cheated and I haven't looked at anyone since. Until I saw you."

"What an idiot. Her, not you. Dirk cheated too. I caught him myself red-handed. Seriously, you date a detective and try to hide something?"

He burst out laughing. Her sense of humor was just one more thing that could be added to the growing list of things he found attractive about her. He pulled her in close for another kiss and held nothing back this time. He wanted her to know he was serious about her. Her body molded perfectly to his as if they were made for each other. He knew they had to be getting back soon, so he reluctantly ended the kiss. Neither spoke but she took his hand and they walked back to the beach to pack their things. Once they were back on the boat, she thanked him for such an incredible day.

"I am glad you brought me here. At first I was disappointed we didn't go to Picnic Island, but now we have our own picnic spot." She was using *we* and *ours* as if it was the most natural thing in the world, and it thrilled him. He gave her a quick kiss on the forehead, then cranked the boat to head back to Key West, and back to reality.

A bit later after arriving back home, Val stretched out on her bed with her computer. She was feeling relaxed after taking a shower and washing away the salt and sand of the day with Reed. She couldn't help smiling as she remembered the kisses and the silly things they teased each other about. Her thoughts began to stray about him in this very bed next to her and she had to snap herself out of it. She had work to do.

She opened her laptop and checked her email. As promised, Al Foster had sent her the pictures he took that day at the first crime scene. She looked closely at the first half dozen or so and saw nothing out of the ordinary. Pictures of police officers walking in and out of the woods, a couple shots of Val talking with Detective Morris, Delaney standing by the Coroner's van. She scanned a few more pictures of the crowd being held back by yellow crime scene tape when she spotted him in the very back of the crowd. She couldn't be sure it was him, so she enlarged the picture. She had a strange feeling about him when she met him, and here he was in the photos of both crime scenes. She didn't know how, but this man definitely played a part in this and she was going to figure out how, so she was going to church in the morning.

Her eyes were growing heavy so she closed her laptop and set it on her bedside table. She fell asleep rather quickly. She dreamed all night of a handsome man, and a swing over sparkling blue water.

Chapter 14

"Tell me everything," Delaney demanded as Val answered her cell phone Sunday morning.

"Damn it Delaney, do you know what time it is?"

"It's 7:30, time for you to get up, or did Reed keep you up last night?"

Valerie laughed despite her grouchiness. "Reed is not here, nor did he keep me up last night. My sunburn kept waking me up though."

"Uh-oh. You didn't get sun burnt in unusual places did you?"

"You're impossible!"

"I'm just wondering how it went."

"It was wonderful. We had a great time, the food and wine were delicious and he is one heck of a kisser. Does that satisfy your curiosity?"

"I was hoping for some juicier details."

"That's as juicy as it got, and if there were juicier details, I wouldn't tell you."

"Party pooper."

"Pervert."

They both laughed. Val asked how Rick was doing and Delany assured her that he was well on the road to recovery if last night was an indication. Delaney never minded sharing details, and although Val could care less, she loved her anyway. That was just her best friend's way. They said their goodbyes and she had just put the phone down and turned over when she heard someone knocking at her front door. What the hell? Couldn't she sleep in at least one damn day of the week? She got up, pulled on her robe and headed downstairs. Before she could get to the door, there was another knock.

"I'm coming," she yelled frustrated. She reached the door and looked through the peephole. It was Reed. She looked like a hot mess, and here he was standing at her front door looking like a golden male model holding a large paper bag. She opened the door a crack.

"Good Morning beautiful."

"I am not beautiful this early in the morning," she grumbled.

"I brought breakfast. Can I come in?" he asked with a hopeful expression.

She opened the door wider. How could she resist a man who brought her food?

He walked by and gave her forehead a quick kiss. Even though it warmed her heart, she was glad it was her forehead. She had not had time to brush her teeth.

"Wow, this place is nothing like I imagined," he commented looking around. "Of course, I have never been on a houseboat, so I guess I didn't know what to expect."

"It's not fancy, but it's home sweet home. Whatcha got in that bag?" she asked inhaling incredible scents as he walked by her to place the bag on the counter.

"Bagels, bacon, fresh fruit and OJ."

"Breakfast of champions. Let me make some coffee. Would you like a cup?"

"Never touch the stuff."

"I can't function without it."

"Good to know, for future reference," he left the meaning open to imagination. He pulled the food out and placed everything on the table as she got the plates and utensils. She put cream in her coffee as he poured the orange juice. They worked around each other as if they had done it for years. Finally, they sat down at the table.

"This was really sweet of you, even though I was ready to kill whoever it was that was knocking on my door," she said between bites of bacon.

"Did I wake you?"

"No, Delaney had that distinct pleasure. She called right before you knocked."

"I'm sorry," he apologized.

"Don't take it personally. I am a major grouch in the morning."

"Another good thing to remember," he said with a wink.

"So, what brings you over this morning?"

"You."

"Me?"

"Yes you. I wanted to see if you were as beautiful in the morning as I have imagined you are."

She rolled her eyes while smiling, "Sorry to disappoint."

"You don't," he replied quietly as he stared at her across the table. The look sent shivers down her spine. "So what are you doing today?"

"Going to church, want to go?" Reed looked up with surprise.

"I'm not exactly dressed for church," referring to his shorts, Guy Harvey shirt, and flip-flops. "I wasn't aware you were the religious type."

"Good instincts Lieutenant. I am going because I have a lead to check up on in my murder cases."

"A lead, in a double murder, at a church?" he asked incredulously.

She told him of her suspicions, and then said, "I need to get dressed. Are you sure you don't want to run home, change, and go with me?"

"I'll take a rain check. You go ahead and get dressed, and I'll clean up this mess."

"There's no need for you to do that. I can do it when I get home."

"I have nothing better to do. Go, I know how to clean a kitchen."

She dressed quickly in a sundress and sandals, brushed her hair and pulled it back with a clip. She brushed her teeth and applied two coats of mascara and some nude lip gloss. She looked demure enough for church she supposed. She headed back downstairs.

The kitchen looked spotless and she saw Reed with his back to her at the sink. "There was really no need for this, but thank you," she said, causing him to turn around. He eyed her up and down and whistled.

"You look beautiful Detective Mason."

She felt her face warming from a blush. She picked her phone up, dropping it into her purse. He was suddenly hugging her from behind, causing her to go weak in the knees. She turned into his hug and immediately felt his lips on hers. She could feel herself drifting away, and she had no desire to come back. His kisses turned her bones into heated liquid. She just wanted to forget the case she was working on, it would be there this afternoon. No ... she owed it to these girls and their families to figure this out before anyone else got hurt. Slowly she pulled away from him placing her forehead against his chin.

"You better get going," he said in a voice that was raw with passion.

She was more than a little breathless, so she could barely speak, much less think straight enough to get her purse and walk out the door. It took a couple of seconds to remember where she was.

He walked out behind her and she locked the door, then they walked down the dock. He stopped beside her car and she turned to him to say she would call him after she got home. He again had her completely engulfed in his arms and a kiss before she knew what was happening. This time he kept it a lot lighter than the last one. "See you in a bit beautiful." He walked over, got in his car and drove away.

With shaky hands, she put the car in drive and pulled out of her parking space. She could use prayer right now to get her there in one piece as discombobulated as she felt. The drive to Big Pine was quick. She had to drive by both scenes to get to the church, and it gave her a sad feeling. She arrived at the same time as Detective Morris and his wife were getting out of their car. He was genuinely surprised to see her.

"I am so glad you decided to come today," he said walking towards her. If he knew the real reason she was here he wouldn't be so glad, she thought. He introduced his wife to Valerie and she felt an odd sense of comfort shaking the woman's hand. She reminded her a little of her mother, having the same hairstyle and color. They would be about the same age if her mom had lived.

"I have heard a bit about you honey," Mrs. Morris said in a soft southern drawl.

"I certainly hope it was the good stuff," Valerie replied with a genuine smile.

"Of course, let's go in and get a seat. It's dreadfully hot out here," she suggested taking Valerie by the arm and leading her up the stairs of the church. It seemed she had forgotten her husband standing there. He trailed behind as if he was used to it.

They walked inside and took seats about halfway to the front of the sanctuary. Several people came over to greet them and inquire about Valerie. Detective Morris explained that she was a co-worker that he had invited to join them today. The other parishioners were very friendly, and greeted her warmly. She could see Pastor Lockhart and Assistant Pastor Cross at the first pew shaking hands, and making their way towards the back. When they finally reached the pew Valerie and the Morris's were on, they both looked surprised to see Valerie.

"I'm sorry detective, but I cannot remember your name," Pastor Lockhart said as he approached Valerie.

"Valerie Mason," she replied extending her hand for a shake.

"That's right. It's good to see you here today."

"Sometimes, people can surprise us," Pastor Cross interjected. He eyed Valerie with curiosity and shook her hand. Her father always said you could tell a lot about a man from his handshake. His was firm indicating to her a show of strength. Pastor Lockhart's was the opposite. His handshake was very vigorous, but was a little over the top, indicating to her that he was not as sincere as he wanted people to believe.

The piano player began playing a hymn in the front of the church to let people know that it was almost time to begin the services, so both pastors hurried along to greet the rest of the people who had filled the remaining pews.

When the services began, Valerie waited patiently until Pastor Lockhart was deeply enthralled in his own sermon, preaching to anyone who was in hearing distance, and probably a few outside the church too, as loud as he seemed to be. He was going on about sinning and the price that you pay for those sins. Typical hellfire and brimstone. We are all going to die and go straight to hell if we don't change our ways. She decided now would be a good time to go search for something; she just wasn't sure what it was. Pastor Cross was seated directly behind Pastor Lockhart, and Valerie could not see him clearly.

She asked Mrs. Morris where the ladies room was and excused herself. She walked back the way they had come into the vestibule and looked around. The men's room was on the left side of the entrance and the ladies room was on the right. She could see a hallway that was beside the women's bathroom and looked down it and saw several doorways, which were likely the offices of the pastors and business affairs. She decided to walk down that way to see if there was anything worth looking at. About halfway down the hall she saw a bulletin board on the wall. She gave it a passing glance, but then caught something out of the corner of her eye that made her stop dead in her tracks. It was a picture of a group of young women, and her sister was among them. What the hell? Was her sister here? The names of the women were listed below the picture, but her sister's name was listed as Tammy Porter.

"Can I help you with something Detective?" Pastor Cross asked, startling Valerie.

"Ummm no. I just came out of the bathroom and saw the bulletin board and thought I would see what activities you have going on here." She had to think fast on her feet for that one.

"As you can see, we don't have many things scheduled right now, because this time of year it starts getting too hot for the softball games and such. Many of our parishioners are getting older, so we have to be thoughtful of these things."

"Well these women are certainly young enough."

"They are not actually members of the church. They are women in a shelter that our church helps run in Key West made possible by donations from our church members."

"Oh, that sounds very charitable."

"That's what we do, we are a church." He sounded as if he was losing patience with her. "Shall we return to the sanctuary and hear what's left of the sermon?"

A retort was on the tip of her tongue to tell him if he had wanted to hear the sermon he should have stayed in there and listened to it, instead of coming out here to spy on her, but she swallowed it back. She followed him back in to hear music playing, and she guessed the service was almost over. She sat in her seat another ten minutes squirming like a five year old.

She had to find out several things. First, if her sister was at the women's shelter and if so, why she was there? Second, if she was somehow mixed up in anything dangerous, and last but not least, if Val's suspicions about the assistant pastor were correct, was she in danger from him? It was a good thing her sister was not going by her real name, for whatever reason. She was trying to remember her conversation with her sister from last week, but the call had been so broken up with static, it had been hard to understand most of what she was saying.

Finally, the pastor called for the dismissal prayer and then everyone started leaving. Valerie was trying to make her way through the crowds of people to the front door only to be stopped by people wanting to shake her hand and tell her how glad they were she had come today.

On her way out the door she noticed the same pamphlet that Pastor Lockhart gave the receptionist at the office the other day. She grabbed one and slid it in the side pocket of her purse. Detective Morris caught up with her and told her that he and his wife would like to take her to lunch, but she told him she had other plans for the afternoon. Thanking both of them, she finally made her way out the front door.

She hurried to her car and was on her way back to Key West with a sigh of relief and frustration. She had come here today hoping to get answers, but left with even more questions. As she came onto the island, she made a decision to visit the women's shelter. She needed to know if her sister was here.

She pulled up to a small pink and gray painted house. It was very well taken care of and had lovely flowers planted all around the edges of the yard. Walking up the front porch, she suddenly felt a knot form in her stomach. Given the history with her sister, she didn't know what to expect.

It was obvious by the fact that Brianna was using an alias that she didn't want anyone knowing that she was here or who she was. Why? She was so sick of questions that had no answers. She rang the doorbell and a middle-aged woman answered. "Hi, can I help you?"

"Yes ma'am. I am Detective Valerie Mason with the Monroe County Sheriff's Department." She showed her badge and ID.

"My name is Holly Stanfield. I run the shelter. What can I do for you detective?"

"I am looking for a lady by the name of Tammy Porter. I was told she may be a guest here."

"I hope she is not in any trouble."

"No not that I know of. I have helped her out in the past and just thought I would check in on her to see how she is doing."

"I'm sorry. I wish I could help, but she didn't check in last night. That is not all that unusual here though. The women come and go as they please and are welcome to as long as they don't bring any trouble through the door. I have to say I thought that Tammy is turning out to be one of our most successful residents. She has really cleaned up her act and is taking classes at the community college to become a counselor to help other women." Valerie must have had a look of utter shock on her face because Holly asked "Is everything ok?"

"I am just ... very glad for her. If she returns can you please tell her to call me at the number on this card?" Even though Brianna had her cell phone number, she gave her a card from the office so not to raise any questions.

"I'd be happy to."

"Thank you for your time."

Val started to walk away when Holly called out to her, "Detective, can you do me a favor?"

"Sure."

"One of the girls has not checked in for several days. Like I said it's not unusual, but for this one it is. She has nobody else but us, and nowhere else to go. She is working hard on getting clean, and she too is taking classes, but I am worried that she might have fallen off the wagon so to speak."

"What's her name? I'll check around and see if I can find out anything."

"Janine Brown. She has been arrested in the past for possession and prostitution so I know she is in your system. I know she sounds bad, but she truly is a sweet girl. She just needs the right guidance. As a matter of fact, Tammy is good friends with her."

"I'll do what I can." She quickly jotted her name down on the back of another one of her business cards. Holly thanked her and Val walked to her car and sat down trying to push back the rising panic. Brianna didn't come back last night and she was friends with a woman that might be missing. She could have stayed with a friend or boyfriend. She would call the shelter in the morning to see if they had heard anything. In the meantime she would run a check on the young girl that Holly had asked about when she got to work in the morning. Maybe if she found her, she would find her sister.

~ ~ ~

He couldn't believe his eyes earlier. Why had the detective chosen today to come to church? He didn't know much about her, but he could tell that she was not a regular attendee at any church, much less this one. Her attention had not been focused on the sermon, and she had got up to go use the restroom, he assumed, towards the end when she could have waited just a few minutes more. He never looked directly at her, but had excellent skills at watching people so no one noticed him doing it. Did she suspect someone in the church of the killings? This could turn out to be a serious problem if he wasn't careful. The last thing he needed was her getting in the way.

A noise behind him caused him to turn around. How he hated to see the condition some of the women in this world they lived in, and the situations they put themselves in. The girl lying on the pallet behind might be finally waking up. He must have given her too much sedative last night because it had taken a while for it to wear off, but she had been really upset and he simply could not handle a crying woman. He reminded himself to be more careful.

His cell phone jangled and he answered. He listened carefully to the person on the other end that needed some help with something that couldn't wait, and agreed to meet him in an hour.

Hanging up, he glanced back over to the girl lying there. She looked peaceful enough. Her dark red hair and fair skin gave her an ethereal angelic look. She was a real beauty, this one.

It must run in her family because her sister, the detective, was a knockout too. It was a shame she had been in that place. He shook his head. Looks could sure be deceiving, but for him, that was a good thing.

Chapter 15

Val could not describe what she was feeling. Frustration? Worry? It had started deep in the recesses of her mind while at church, and had intensified after she left the women's shelter.

Her cell phone rang snapping her out of her thoughts. The caller ID showed Reed's name. She let it go to voice mail and then felt guilty for ignoring it. She would call him back in a while. She really wanted to clear her head and give thought to putting all the pieces together that didn't seem to fit.

She suddenly thought of those kisses they had shared, so on second thought she hit the redial button through her car's sync system. They spoke for several minutes and she agreed to meet with him a little later. She was going to pick up lunch and go to his house.

When she arrived at the boathouse she quickly changed into a tank top and denim cutoff shorts and hurried back down the stairs, slid on a pair of Kino sandals she had left by the front door. She dialed the Surf's Up Shack and ordered lunch. Picking up her purse to give them her credit card number, the church pamphlet fell out of the front pocket. After hanging up the phone she stared at the pamphlet for a few seconds and a memory was struggling to form itself in her mind.

Suddenly she was reminded of the small scrap of paper she had found at the first crime scene. She remembered shoving it into her pants pocket, which were now in the bottom of her hamper. She ran upstairs and dumped her dirty laundry on the foot of her bed. Finding the pants she was looking for, she dug around in the pockets until she found the scrap.

Thank God it was still there. She took it and the church pamphlet and held them side-by-side. It was as if the scrap of paper was a puzzle piece, and if the pamphlet had been missing a piece it would fit right in the center of it. The small piece was part of a picture of a cross with an s-like design around it.

Suddenly her heart began to race with excitement. She now had some confirmation of her suspicions. How did that scrap get out there by the body of a murder victim, unless the Pastor was involved, or at the very least someone that was familiar with the church. Of course, the pamphlets were handed out to people so anyone could have dropped it at any time. She didn't think the latter was the case though. She would concentrate her efforts and investigation on Pastor Cross now. Finally, she was getting somewhere! She began to fear nothing would ever turn up.

She thought about calling Detective Morris but instead she called to leave a message for Agent Giovanni telling him she had some new evidence. She knew she should call Morris too, but what if he slipped up and said something in front of Pastor Lockhart, and he in turn tried to confront Pastor Cross. She needed to see him in person first thing in the morning and tell him that nobody could be told about her suspicions. Right now the only person she wanted to have this information was Agent Giovanni, and of course she knew she could tell Reed.

Trying to balancing her phone on her shoulder and holding it in place with the side of her head while she was locking her front door, she ended up dropping it, and had to scramble to catch it before it fell into the water.

She released a sigh as she caught it. As she was standing back up, someone rounded the corner at the end of the row of houseboats. She had seen legs and shoes, but she had not seen or heard anyone coming down the dock. She walked to that end of the walkway and peered around the corner but there was no one around. Had someone been there watching her or was she losing her mind and being paranoid? Shaking her head she walked back down the dock to the parking lot. It was only a five-minute drive from her place to the sandwich shop.

She stood in line for a couple of minutes adding two bags of chips and sodas to her order after finally making it to the register. Signing the receipt, she turned to leave when she spotted Agent Giovanni at the far end of the counter. He had not spotted her, so she walked towards him. He was picking up a clear bag that had two sandwiches in it. Two for himself? He looked caught off guard to see her.

"Hey there! I thought you would have headed back to the mainland by now."

"I was, but thought I would stay around a couple of days and go over those reports and pictures a little more. There has to be something we're missing."

"You didn't get my message earlier I take it."

"No. I haven't checked my messages this morning."

"I found a small scrap of paper at the first crime scene. It wasn't close to the body, just off the side of the trail where you enter the woods. It really looked like nothing but litter. So I picked it and put it in my pocket to throw it away. I completely forgot about it until today after I picked up a pamphlet at church that made it come to mind. That's because the scrap came from a pamphlet like it. Maybe my suspicions about Pastor Cross are plausible."

145

He looked stunned. "A scrap of paper is not enough evidence to arrest someone on suspicion of murder."

"I know, but I think it tells me I'm on the right track."

"You never can tell. Sometimes we can't see what we're looking for even when it's right in front of us." That was an odd statement.

"Let me know if you find anything."

"Of course."

"Have a good afternoon," he said as he walked away. He turned and glanced back her way briefly to see if she was still there, but she was gone. Once down the street and out of view, the agent pulled out his cellphone. "It's me, I just saw Valerie Mason ... she is taking her investigation in a dangerous direction." He was silent as the person at the end of the line spoke. "I haven't quite figured her out yet. I just hope she doesn't go looking for her sister."

~ ~ ~

Val smiled as she pulled into Reed's driveway. The house was even more beautiful in the daytime than it had been the night she had given him a ride home. It looked like it belonged in the island edition of Garden and Homes Magazine. She reached over and grabbed the sandwiches from the passenger seat and the drinks from the cup holders. After lunch, they were going to stroll downtown and just enjoy the day together.

After ringing the doorbell, she only had to wait a few seconds for Reed to answer. He stood before shirtless causing her heart to skip a beat. Of course, she had seen him shirtless at the beach, but for some reason it felt different. It was a visual that would not leave her for a while. He was holding a shirt in his hand and pulling it over his head he explained that he had taken a shower after working in the yard.

"It looks great, your flowers are beautiful," she complimented.

"Thanks but I feel bad taking the credit. My grandfather did the work, I just do the upkeep." They stepped into coolness of the cottage. Valerie let her eyes adjust to the light change. Then, she fell instantly in love. It was picture perfect. The living room was not big but was just the right size for two. The furniture was overstuffed and looked comfortable.

"Let me give you the grand tour," he offered.

"Please! If the rest of it is as beautiful as this, I can't wait," she agreed enthusiastically.

"Well, of course by now you have guessed you are in the living room. To the left and through the French doors we have the kitchen and dining area. "They walked into a rather spacious kitchen with professional grade appliances. She hoped that meant he liked to cook, because she hated it. The dining area was a booth reminiscent of the fifties era built into the bay windows that overlooked the back yard.

This is gorgeous! Your grandparents had wonderful taste."

"My grandmother designed most of it herself with the exception of one special room. My grandfather had his own ideas for that one."

"Ok, now I'm intrigued."

"Patience, my dear. We will get there eventually." He grinned as he took her by the elbow and led her back into the living room. He motioned to the hallway on the right side of the room and said, "Ladies first."

Coming to the first room on the left he said, "behind door number one, we have the guest room, which is currently full of junk, so I apologize ahead of time" Opening the door she could see he was truthful.

147

There were numerous boxes that held whatever he had failed to unpack when he had moved in, some fishing equipment stood in one corner and various weights and a weight bench was against the far wall. A twin-sized bed was covered with odds and ends. Next door was the guest bathroom. It was small and decorated with ocean colors and a seashell theme. "Last but not least was my grandfather's pride and joy. The master suite."

He opened the door and as Valerie stepped through, she stood speechless. The room was almost an exact replica of Ernest Hemingway's bedroom in his house over on Whitehead Street.

"Oh Reed. This is gorgeous," she said with an awe filled voice. She ran her hand along the end of the bed, and then over the edge of the desk.

"My grandfather was a huge Hemingway fan, so he had replicas made. He spent a lot of time at that house taking pictures for the furniture makers"

"I'm a huge fan too, so this is just..." she struggled to find a word that could describe what she was feeling.

"I know, a little bird told me. I have been dying to show this to you."

A painting of The Whitehead Street home hung over the bed. Another replica painting of The Old Man and the Sea hung over the desk. Directly across from the foot of the bed was a beautiful hand carved fireplace that looked identical to the ones she had seen on tour of the house. It had gas logs in lieu of real ones. It added charm and romance to the space. There were two other pairs of French doors and without waiting for Reed, she crossed the bedroom and opened the first pair. She squealed with delight. The bathroom was also an exact replica of Hemingway's bathroom from the black glass case that held rare seashells, to the corner sink and the lovely built in vanity dressing table for the lady of the house.

Reed leaned against the doorway with his arms crossed over his chest and smiled. It gave him a sense of pride to know Valerie was amazed by everything she was seeing.

"I am in love. I have never seen anything as amazing as this."

"I'm glad you like it, but there is one more thing to show you." He pointed to the other set of French doors close to the fireplace. She practically ran across the room and flung them open. She gasped. There before her was a secret garden. A small patio completely walled off from prying eyes. There was a hot tub surrounded by lush tropical foliage and flowers. Two layback lounge chairs flanked one wall and a swing large enough for two people to lie in was along the other wall.

"Reed you are the luckiest person alive to live here. I thought my houseboat was cool, but this beats anything I have ever seen."

"I am thankful my grandparents chose me to leave it to. My brother was part owner, but he signed his part over to me as long as he could stay here when he visits."

"Your brother must be nuts. If this was mine, I could never give it up."

"Well, since you brought it up, we can work towards that." That stopped her dead in her tracks.

That was a serious statement, and it took a few moments before she replied, "I would only want you for your house."

He cocked one eyebrow and said, "Oh, really? I guess I'll have to give you some other reasons to help you reconsider."

Suddenly she became aware of how close they were to each other. He moved slowly towards her, taking her hand and pulling her inside from the patio. He closed the doors behind her. She leaned against the doors for support, because the way he was looking at her was causing her legs to turn to jelly.

He leaned down and nuzzled her ear and then whispered, "I'm falling in love with you. It's only fair to let you know that." His breath drifted softly across her skin causing her to shiver. He kissed her neck and she felt his stubble-covered jaw rub her shoulder. Her veins suddenly felt as if there was molten lava flowing through them. She put her arms around his neck and stood on her tiptoes so she could reach his mouth. The sheer intensity of her kiss surprised them both and ignited the spark they were both feeling into a full blown five-alarm fire. He pulled her body against him and felt like he could not get close enough. Somehow, in the next few moments in between passion filled kisses, their clothes simply vanished and all at once they were laying on the Hemingway bed looking into each other's eyes.

"I don't think I am falling in love with you," she said, "I know I am." She saw a brief flash of disappointment followed by a darkening of passion in his eyes. She knew he would be a generous lover just by the way he traced kisses from her lips, to her chin, then her collar bone and lower. She ran her fingers through his hair thrilled by the attention he lavished on every square inch of her. Finally, she could take no more and begged him to take her. He rose above her and made love to her, making her feel things she had never felt or even imagined possible.

She could feel the sensation building that would take her to the edge of oblivion. The muscles in Reed's back were tightening and she knew he too was at the precipice with her. She felt as if she exploded into a million pieces and he with her. Slowly she floated down from that place Reed had taken her to and they lay silently in each other's arms. As soon as their breathing had returned to normal, he finally spoke.

"I have never felt anything that incredible in my life. You are an amazing woman, Valerie Mason." He kissed the top of her nose.

"Me either. Literally. I never knew it could feel like that."

He gave her a surprised look. "Really?"

"Let's just say that nobody ever cared about how I felt, only themselves." He picked up her hand and placed it to his lips giving it a kiss. "I can promise you that will never happen again." Teasing her to make her smile he added "I like the little sounds you make and the way you say my name when I..." he didn't get to finish because she smacked him with a pillow. "Oww, what was that for?"

"For embarrassing me, so stop it," she said with a giggle. Her cheeks were bright pink.

"You're sexy when you're embarrassed so I am going to have to make you blush more often."

"I guess you're going to get whacked a lot with pillows then."

"Not if you don't have any to whack me with," he said yanking the pillow from her and throwing it across the room. He quickly grabbed the others from the bed and threw them too before she had a chance to get one of them. She tried to jump up to get one but he grabbed her around her waist and pulled her back down on the bed. He threw his leg over hers so she couldn't escape causing her to giggle and accused him of false imprisonment.

He knew right in that moment that she was going to be his forever, but he would take his time because he didn't want to scare her off. It had been fast for him, but when it's right, it's right. He then proceeded to do the very thing that would make her say his name just the way he wanted to hear it.

~ ~ ~

Although Valerie was content lying in Reed's arms, she felt an overwhelming hunger. She remembered they had left their sandwiches on the counter when they had started the *tour*. She suggested that they go eat, and true to his nature, Reed told her that it was good idea because he was going to need to keep his strength up to keep up with her. She punched him in the arm and he pretended to be in pain holding his arm while watching her put on his T-shirt. It fit her like a mini dress.

"That is certainly my favorite T-shirt from now on. It looks a helluva lot better on you than it does on me." He held her around the waist from behind all the way into the kitchen. Their drinks were watered down from sitting too long, so he poured them both a glass of iced tea. Instead of sitting in the kitchen, they made themselves comfortable on the couch. Val instinctually tucked her legs under her as she sat down. That brought a smile to Reed's face knowing she felt at home. She fit so perfectly into his life.

Val caught him watching her and stopped mid bite. "What?"

"Nothing, just thinking."

"About?"

"Was I chewing with my mouth open or something?"

"Not that I noticed."

"Then what? It's driving me crazy."

"You drive me crazy." He was giving her that look again.

"No you don't. Eat your sandwich," she said pointing her finger at him and smiling. "There's plenty of time for that later. We have a date this afternoon don't forget."

"I haven't forgotten. I was thinking maybe you would like to take a dip in the hot tub later and the drift off to dream in Hemingway's bedroom."

A beautiful smile covered her face and he could tell she was agreeable.

"I would love to." She was quiet for a couple minutes and was picking at her sandwich. "You don't think we are moving too fast do you?"

"Not for me, do you want to slow down? I'm sorry if I seemed pushy by asking you to stay the night." He looked a little pensive.

"No. I just want you to be sure this is what you want. I know what I want."

"What is it you want?"

"This, whatever it is, with you."

"That's exactly what I want too. I can honestly say I have never been as content with any woman as I am with you. I know we haven't known each other long, but my mom has always told me that when I found the right one, I would just know, and I know."

With that last statement for her to think about, they finished their lunch and got dressed. They were headed down to Mallory Square for a little shopping and to watch the sunset from the pier. They stopped outside the front door so Reed could lock up. Her heart was full, and she was content and happy for the first time in a long time. Funny how a little afternoon delight could change your whole attitude. She could just hear Delaney's snide comments and jokes. She smiled despite herself at the reaction her friend would have to learn of her new relationship.

153

Grabbing her hand, they walked towards the end of the street so they could cross over to Duvall and head to Mallory Square. Peace and happiness was evident on both their faces. At least for the moment. They walked along the sidewalk and talked about where they would eat for dinner, stopping in shops along the way, laughing at the sayings on the front of the T-shirts that hung in the windows of so many of the shops. When it got close to sunset, they picked a spot on the pier and sat down, and even though they were surrounded by people, they felt as if they were in their own little world. As the huge orange ball was dipping slowly into the ocean, Reed kissed Val lightly on the lips. He was just about to tell her he loved her when his cell phone rang. After looking down at the caller ID, he told Val he had to take the call. It was his father and he generally did not call him unless it was important.

She looked around at all the performers and the crowds gathered around each one. She decided to see what the different artists had to offer. There was stained glass depicting various sunsets and ocean life, hand blown wineglasses, paintings, and clothing crafted by some of the finest artists on the island. There were coconuts carved and painted to look like pirates, and wine bottles that had been made into lamps with tiny clear lights in them. This was one of the reasons she loved living in Key West, it was a town full of talented people who loved sharing their passions.

Reed found her in the crowd after a few minutes and apologized. "I'm sorry, but my parents had a stove catch on fire. They managed to put the fire out, even before the fire department arrived, but they asked if I could come and help them clean up the mess it made. If not, they will have to stay closed tomorrow."

"Oh wow, I am glad everything and everyone is ok."

"Me too. From what my Dad said, there's not much damage, but there is a big mess from the smoke and the fire extinguisher spray."

"Ok, let's go."

"You don't have to help."

"It's no big deal. I have nothing better to do."

Thanking her, he grabbed her hand and they headed towards the intersection that would lead them to the restaurant, which was a brief five-minute walk from the pier. Arriving at the back door, they could hear Reed's dad cussing like a drunken sailor, and his mother chastising him for using such language. Reed actually blushed under his big grin.

"Sorry about that" he said sheepishly as he looked towards Valerie.

"No need, I have a dad too you know, and believe me that is tame compared to what he would be saying."

As they stepped through the back door both of his parents smiled and his dad's face went from pissed off to a friendly demeanor.

Reed introduced everyone. His parents were gracious and seemed excited to meet her, as well as thankful for the extra pair of hands. They asked questions of each other having a get to know you session, and Val learned their names were James and Sarah. They began wiping down counters and walls, mopping floors, and scrubbing pans that weren't ruined from the fire.

The stove was a loss, so Reed and his father moved it out of the kitchen into the alley. James would call the city tomorrow and arrange to have the waste management company haul it away. They had been hoping to salvage it, but they would have to do the best they could with the remaining two stoves until a new one could be delivered. It would probably take two to three days to get one here from Miami.

Valerie and Sarah had prepared everyone a late night snack and the men showed their appreciation by devouring the sandwiches and sweet tea.

"We are so glad Reed brought you by. I just wish it hadn't been to help us clean up a near catastrophe," Sarah said with a genuine smile.

"It was really no problem. Like I told Reed, I had nothing better to do. But, I do have to go to work in the morning so I need to get going. I didn't realize it was almost midnight. It was really nice meeting you both."

"Nice meeting you too, and don't be a stranger," James told her, and then turning to Reed said "Stop keeping her to yourself."

"Yes sir," he replied as his dad slapped him on the back. He waked Valerie out to the sidewalk. They were both feeling the disappointment of not being together tonight. "I'm so sorry we have to change our plans."

"Don't be. Your parents need your help and I never had a chance to go home and get my clothes. There will be other nights. You'll probably get sick of me."

"Not a chance in hell of that happening. Let me tell my parents that I'll be back as soon as I walk you to your car."

"There's no need for you to walk me to my car."

"Are you sure?"

"I'll be fine. Stay and help your parents set up for tomorrow."

He wrapped his arms around her waist and pulled her in close. "Today has been incredible." Reed looked into her eyes, and then lowered his face to hers for a bone-melting kiss. She didn't know why this man had this effect on her, but she was sure glad he did. "Are you sure you don't want me to walk you to your car?"

"Yes, I can handle myself."

"I know you can, but I am trying to be a gentleman and walking you to your car will give me another excuse to kiss you goodbye."

"Who said you needed an excuse?"

"I like the way you think Detective Mason."

This time, she stood on her tiptoes and kissed him. She hoped her kisses had the same effect on him as his did on her. She was pretty damn sure they did.

"Be careful," he said with his forehead pressed against hers.

"I will." She started to walk away when he called out. She turned to look at him. She walked back to him and kissed him. They held onto to each other's hands until she had moved far enough away that they pulled apart.

He stood for a while and watched her walk until she reached the end of the sidewalk. She looked back waved and blew him a kiss, then turned right on the sidewalk that would take her to his house. He knew he shouldn't worry, she was a cop and had been trained in self-defense. His house was only a few blocks over so she would be there in no time. He took a deep breath and could not seem to wipe the smile from his face that she had put there. Turning, he walked back into the Bistro to find his parents sitting at a table staring at him.

"What?" he asked, suddenly feeling as if he was sixteen years old again.

"She is very nice, and lovely to boot," his mother teased in a singsong voice.

"Yes, she is," he replied stretching his long legs out and leaning back in his chair. "I have finally found the one."

"Son, as great as we think she is, I hardly think a couple of dates could tell you she's the one," his Dad surmised.

"Mom always told me, when you find the girl you want to be with for the rest of your life, you'll just know it, and for me, it's Valerie."

Both his parents looked a little astonished but happy. Reaching over and grabbing her son's hand, his mom said, "We're happy for you son. You deserve a sweet girl like her."

His dad agreed. "One things for sure, we'll have good looking grandkids." They all shared a chuckle over that and sat for a while longer talking about life, love and dreams of what could be. They didn't realize that at that very moment, Reed and Valerie's future was about to take an uncertain turn.

~ ~ ~

A misty fog had rolled in off the ocean tonight. It was produced from the storm earlier in the day combined with the humidity of the evening. It hung in the air and made the walk to her car seem lonely and dark. The street was eerily quiet after the last few weeks of loud partiers on Spring break. She was spooked without explanation and was beginning to wish that she had let Reed walk her to her car. The few sounds that could be heard were distant, such as music from a bar that must have still had a few patrons not ready to call it a night. She could hear a dog barking and of course the hum of air conditioners that were never turned off here in the tropics.

She had walked about two blocks when the sound of an engine could be heard approaching and she looked up to notice that it was going about fifteen miles an hour. The car was at enough of a distance that she could cross the street safely. Reed's house was on the opposite side of the street than she had been walking on. Now, the car was passing by her and as it passed under a street lamp, so she glanced over quickly. It looked familiar. It came to a stop at a stop sign then turned left onto a side street. Boy, was she jittery tonight.

A few seconds later, she heard the engine again, only this time it was coming towards her from behind. She picked up her pace and told herself to get a grip. The driver was probably lost and had taken the wrong route. Some of these streets were one way, and could be confusing if you weren't from around here.

She kept waiting for the car to pass her, but it never did. It seemed to be following her. She suddenly wished she had her gun. She neglected to bring it with her, because she didn't think she would need it. She almost never went anywhere without it, but she didn't want to be reminded of work while she was with Reed, and had left it in her car. She wouldn't make that mistake again.

Slowly, the car pulled up beside her. She glanced over and to her surprise, it came to a complete stop. Behind the wheel sat the Pastor. Now she remembered. It was the car at the church.

"Need a ride detective?"

"No, I'm fine. My car is right up ahead." A few seconds passed as he glanced around and then uncovered a gun lying on the seat beside him. "I insist."

She tried to ascertain her chances of running, but none of the shops in this part of town were open, and the streets seemed so deserted that there was no reason to yell for help, because no one would hear. She was utterly alone and at his mercy, especially now that he had the gun pointed at her. Without her service weapon, she was left with no choice.

She grabbed the door handle and reluctantly got in.

"Hand me your cell phone." She reached in her pocket, pulled it out, and handed it to him. "You look like you have seen a ghost detective."

Realization fell down on her like a lead weight, and she could feel her hope dwindling for getting out of this. She had to keep her head straight and keep her cool. She could do this, she just had to think.

"No, not a ghost. Just a liar and murderer."

Chapter 16

The night was black as ink, and the fog bank rolling in made the light from the stars seem non-existent. "Damn this fog" he muttered in annoyance.

"Where are we going?" Val asked with no expectation of an honest answer.

"To a quiet place of sanctuary."

"The church?"

He laughed at her. "The church is no sanctuary. There are too many hypocrites. People who come on Sunday morning, profess their faith, and live like heathens the rest of the week, always walking that thin line between Saturday night sinning and Sunday morning service."

"Given that you have murdered innocent women, what does that make you?"

Flustered and angered by her question, he answered with a raised voice, "I have never committed murder! Those young women were anything but innocent. I was simply saving them before they died so they would not spend eternity in hell. They were harlots, flaunting themselves for men, and using drugs and alcohol to numb the pain of their own shame. I give them a chance to repent before they pay for their sins."

Now Valerie was just as pissed as he seemed. "The first woman you *murdered* was a waitress not a *harlot*. Nor was she a drug user or an alcoholic," she seethed.

"She wore tempting clothing to lure men to buy the food and drinks where she worked. It's the same thing, using her body to make a profit."

"So where is your sense of forgiveness for people *Pastor?*" She spat out that last word knowing he was not worthy of the title. "Who gave you the right to judge?"

"The wages of sin is death ... look it up sometime Detective."

"I don't have to. It's in Romans. I can quote scripture right along with you, you're not the only one who knows the Bible."

"I must say, I'm impressed. But even the devil knows the good word. If you have studied the Bible, you know that I am not doing anything but the Lord's work."

"You are taking things out of the Bible and using them to fit your own agenda, Not God's. I am quite positive that the sixth commandment is Thou shall not kill, and he meant it for everyone, including you."

"Ezekiel 18:20, the soul that sinneth, shall die"

"Yeah, and II Corinthians 5:10, for we all must appear before the judgment seat of Christ. That includes you, and if for one minute you think you will not be judged by God, then just know when you are caught, you *will* be judged by a jury of your peers."

"I am done arguing with you. You're a fool who knows nothing about what I do and why I do it."

"Oh, I know why you do it. You're a damn psycho!"

He backhanded her across the face, and whether or not it was a good idea, she came undone and began beating him with both of her fists, his mistake for not pulling over to bond her hands and feet. He also wished he had taped her smart mouth shut. The sudden attack caused him to lose control of the car and sent it swerving into a spin on the dirt road he had turned onto from the main highway. Thankfully, there was no other traffic on this road. She wasn't wearing her seatbelt, so when the car came to a sudden, jolting stop against a trio of palm trees, she hit her head on the dash. Dazed, it took a couple of seconds to gather her wits and realize they had finally crashed. She felt a sticky wetness on her forehead and reaching up, she found blood trickling out of a fresh cut. She noticed her arm had a gash on it too, and was bleeding pretty heavily.

"Are you crazy? You almost killed us both." He was fumbling around trying to remove his seatbelt. Now was her opportunity to run. When she looked around though, the door had been crunched up against the trees on her side, so there was no escape. Find the gun, was her next thought. She knew it was probably no longer in the seat after the crash, and apparently he was thinking the same thing. He opened his door to get out, and found it wedged between the seat and the door jam.

She could see he was bleeding from the nose, and a cut above his eye. He quickly wiped away the blood on the sleeve of his shirt. "Get out ... now." he growled.

Slowly, so she could glance around in search of anything she could use as a weapon, she scooted across both seats and got out on the driver's side. There was nothing. Damn! She felt dizzy when she stood up, and she realized she was probably suffering from a concussion compounded by loss of blood. She put her hands on her knees and tried to stop the nausea and dizziness sweeping over her. She could see him getting something from the trunk of the car. He must have felt sure she wasn't going anywhere. Walking back to where she was bent over, he grabbed her by the arm and she winced in pain from a cut on her arm.

"I guess we walk from here, thanks to you, so if you're hurt, it's your own fault."

Valerie remained silent during the walk which was about a half mile down the road from where the car had crashed. She didn't know if she was going to make it, and a couple of times thought she might pass out causing her to stumble. He would quickly snatch her back into an upright position, making her arm throb and bleed even more. She stumbled once and fell to her knees and she could hear him cursing her under his breath. That time though, he let her rest several seconds before putting the gun in her back and telling her to move.

Eventually, she could see an old bridge that was not used anymore. A newer one had replaced it long ago. He directed her underneath the bridge and she could see an old building that was nothing more than a rundown shack. More than likely, it had been used by the old bridge keepers as a place to sleep when doing shift work. Years ago, it was easier to work for the week and then go home after than it was to travel back and forth. When they reached the door, he handed her a key and had her unlock the lock that was hanging from a hasp hinge. Once unlocked, they walked through the door of a musty smelling room. He flipped a switch near the door but the light output was very dim.

He shoved her towards a nasty mattress stained with things she would rather not think about. She could hear a scraping noise on the other side of the room, but the light didn't reach quite that far, so she could not see what was making the noise. It was probably rats. It could be a raccoon or feral cat too, as they were plentiful here.

Commanding her to turn around, he tied her hands behind her back so tight that she winced from the pain. It wouldn't be too long until they went numb. At least the bleeding from her arm wound had slowed down some. He then forced her to sit and tied her ankles together with another piece of the same rope. Without saying another word to Valerie, he turned and walked back out the only door. She could hear him replace the lock through the hasp and snap it together.

Now what? When was he coming back and when he did, was he planning to kill her like he did the other two girls? She had to think of something fast because she was feeling panic beginning to rise up threatening to overtake her.

Taking a deep breath to steady her nerves, she blew it out slowly. Think Valerie, and let those cop instincts kick in. Her nerves finally steadied enough that she could think clearly and began to form a plan. It wasn't much of one, but it was all she had. When he returned, she was taking the preacher to church, and not in the literal sense.

Chapter 17

Reed had never experienced a night of sleeplessness like he had last night. He had arrived home around two-thirty a.m. only to find Valerie's mustang still parked in his driveway.

He walked around the perimeter of his house to see if she might be waiting on the back lanai for him to return. There was no one there. He scanned the yard and could see nothing or no one out there. Where the hell could she be? Unlocking the back door and walking in, he called out her name a couple of times, half expecting her to answer but knowing she didn't have a key to his house.

Silence.

Searching through his pockets for his cellphone, he quickly dialed her number, but it went straight to voice mail. Dozens of thoughts were swimming through his mind. Should he call the office and have people out looking for her? She can take care of herself, but even cops need backup sometimes. If nothing is wrong, then where is she, and why would she have left her car here? If she were in trouble, wouldn't she have called him? What if she couldn't call because she was hurt or something worse?

Stop thinking like that! He paced back and forth for several minutes then decided to go down to the station and report her missing. Grabbing his car keys off the hook by the back door, he walked out to his garage. Damn, her car was parked behind his. He wouldn't be able to back his car out. The driveway was only wide enough for one vehicle.

He wasn't about to call his dad for a ride because he was probably already asleep by now.

So was everybody he knew. He went back into his garage and pulled his bike down from the wall. It was a beachcomber and hadn't been ridden for about a year, but it would have to do. The station Valerie worked from was only 3 miles from here so it wouldn't take him that long.

The entire way there he couldn't keep his mind off the what-ifs. He found himself pedaling faster. He dropped the bike on the small piece of lawn that was big enough to hold a flagpole and monument to fallen officers and practically ran to the front door. As soon as he entered, the officer at the front desk looked up. It was a buddy of his Thomas Sutton.

"Hey Reed, what are you doing here this time of night, or morning I should say?"

"I need to speak to whoever is in charge tonight. I am not sure who is on schedule."

"Oh, that would be Lt. Jackson. He's in the back. Hopefully not asleep." He added with a chuckle. Noticing that Reed didn't laugh or even smile, he became concerned. "What's going on Reed?"

"Hopefully nothing," he said heading down the hall. Charlie Jackson used to be Marine patrol until he had a severe knee injury that placed him behind a desk for the rest of his career. Knocking on the door that had been left open, he caught Jackson rubbing his eyes.

"Reed, what brings you in?"

"Valerie Mason is missing."

"What?" Jackson sat straight up in his chair. "Why do you think she is missing?"

Not knowing where to begin he rubbed his temples. He told him everything from Val's suspicions about the Reverend on Big Pine down to her leaving his parents restaurant earlier and him coming home to find her car still parked in his driveway.

Picking up the phone, Jackson called dispatch and told them to immediately contact all officers in the area to be on the lookout for Valerie. "You know technically we can't say she is missing until she has been gone twenty four hours, but because we work with her and know her we'll go ahead and look around," he told Reed as he hung up. Standing up and coming around the desk he patted Reed on the shoulder and said, "We'll find her, don't worry." Until he had her back in his arms that is exactly what he would do.

As the sun came up, Reed set out to show her picture around. He wasn't having much luck at all. The problem was there were people who knew her and had seen her, just not last night. He continued down the sidewalk with the picture he had printed out from the online yearbook on the sheriff department's website. Why he had never thought to look her up that way after he met her that day in the Big Pine substation? The picture of her did not do her justice, although it was still a beautiful one.

He was tired, hot and dying of thirst. He stopped at a small drink stand and ordered a bottle of water. As he stood there waiting, he saw a man coming out of a nearby alley between two hotels. He had the look of either a homeless person, or a scraggly fisherman. His clothes were worn with his shorts showing a few flashes of weathered skin through the holes they had. His salt and pepper hair looked very unkempt and matched his chest length beard. He was carrying a bucket and a cane pole, a fishing pole fashioned from a long stalk of bamboo, and very popular in Florida. Not many people used them in saltwater, but if that's all you had, Reed guessed it would work. Beside him a Golden retriever strayed along and every so often looked up at the old man with loyalty. Reed figured they were a perfect pair.

"Excuse me sir, have you seen this woman?" Reed asked holding the picture up as he approached the pair. The old man looked a bit confused that someone might be asking him something important. Most people probably ignored him and pretended he didn't exist. He smiled a near toothless grin.

"Sure she gives me and Barney doughnuts and coffee in the morning sometimes."

"When was the last time you saw her?"

"Last night."

Reed's hopes soared. "Where did you see her? What was she doing?"

"Well you see, me and Barney here was just getting ready to fall asleep, and I thought I heard someone talking. I looked around the corner to see who it was because Barney can be real territorial and all. I didn't want anyone going down our alley and getting attacked.

Reed looked down at the dog who seemed to be smiling with his tongue hanging out the side of his mouth. Yeah, real vicious animal there.

"Anyway," the man continued, "it was the nice police lady and she was talking to somebody in a car. She got in after a couple of minutes; I guess she needed a ride. When they passed by I saw that preacher fella that helps out at the soup kitchen sometimes was driving. Me and Barney love eating there. The food is always..." Reed tuned him out. Why would Valerie accept a ride with anyone, especially someone she suspected of murder? What had she gotten herself into? Had the pastor figured that she suspected him and come after her? He would never forgive himself for not walking her back to her car if anything bad happened to her.

"We really like the coconut cake..." The old man was still rambling on. Snapping back from his thoughts, Reed opened his wallet and gave the man a twenty-dollar bill.

"Thanks for your help. Take this and get yourself a decent lunch."

"Thanks mister. By the way, my name is Andy if you ever need anything else," he said eyeing the money as if he had just won the lottery.

His name was Andy and the dog was Barney? Reed would have burst out laughing if the situation wasn't so serious. He could find no humor at the moment. He hurried to the corner of his parent's bistro and borrowed their jeep. He had a key on his ring for it so he would call them and leave them a message so they didn't worry it had been stolen. He was quickly on his way to Big Pine. He called the dispatch to tell them where he was headed and what he had found out. His next call was to Detective Morris asking him to meet him at the church. The normally short drive seemed to be taking forever, but he soon arrived at the church, miraculously given the way he had been driving. He shoved the gear shifter into park and jumped out.

Approaching the front door, he found it locked. He jogged back down the front steps checking the left side first and finding only windows. He went back around the front and then to the right side of the building to see if there were other entrances to try. There were two doors but both were locked also. There was a white Toyota parked in the lot so he knew someone was here. Once again he went back to the front door and pounded on it with his fist. Waiting several seconds, he pounded again.

He thought he could hear someone coming towards the front door, then heard it being unlocked from the inside. Pastor Cross stood before him.

"What is the urgency sir?"

Grabbing the pastor by the shoulders, he shoved him backwards.

"Where is she you son of a bitch?"

"I advise you to keep your hands off me. Where is who?" his voice was calm but threatening.

"Don't play stupid. Where is Valerie Mason?"

"Detective Mason? I don't know, why would I?"

Reed lunged forward again and the pastor spoke a little louder than before.

"I've warned you once, do not come at me again." That was an odd statement coming from a preacher.

"If you don't tell me where she is I'm going to ..." Reed was interrupted by commotion from behind him.

"Lt. Stone, what in the world is going here?"

"This so called preacher took Valerie last night, I'm trying to find out where he took her."

Morris' face registered shock. "Why in the world would he kidnap Valerie?"

"Because he is a killer, not a preacher."

Both Morris and Cross looked stunned for a couple seconds and no one spoke.

"That's ridiculous. This man is not a killer," Morris argued looking from Reed to Cross as if he wasn't sure about what he had just claimed.

"We have a witness that saw her get into a car with him."

"A witness saw her get into the car with me?" Cross asked.

"Yes, he said Valerie got into the car with the pastor. Somehow you found out that Valerie was on to you, and now you have taken her."

Cross looked pale, and Reed guessed the good Reverend knew it was over for him.

"You're right Lieutenant. I'm not a preacher." This revelation stunned everyone into silence once again. "My name is Matt Franklin. Agent Matt Franklin, with the FBI. I was sent here to watch over the real suspect. He might have committed two murders here so far, but we have reason to believe, and the evidence, that ties him to eighteen other murders over a thirty-year span. There may be more, but some of the cases are older, and there isn't much evidence, DNA wise anyway. We are aware that Detective Mason suspected me, because of her talking with a fellow agent of mine Tony Giovanni."

Detective Morris asked "Just who is that you have under surveillance, and why wasn't I notified?"

"Detective we have spent years building a case against him and we couldn't chance anybody doing something that might tip him off. I'm sorry we had to keep all of it completely covert."

"You still haven't told me who you suspect."

"Reverend Lockhart, and we haven't seen him since last night. He used the church's car to take used clothing to the homeless shelter in Key West but never returned with the car."

"If you had him under surveillance then you should know where he disappeared to," Reed chimed in.

"It's not that simple Detective. We tried tailing him, but last night with the fog being as thick as it was, Agent Giovanni lost him. He can't exactly tailgate him everywhere he goes, we had to give him some room so he didn't get suspicious. We called his house and there was no answer. I went over there this morning and nobody was home. I have his wife's cell phone number and apparently she is out of town visiting her sister."

Detective Morris sat down on the back pew trying to gather his thoughts. Donald Lockhart ... a serial killer? Good Lord, what was this world coming to when the preacher you have heard sermon after sermon from over the past few years could be this evil?

"We have to get things rolling quickly." Agent Franklin suggested. He pulled out a phone and called to have several agents come to Big Pine. The sheriff's department was ready and more than willing to assist in finding one of their own. Reed was trying to tamper down his fear and spoke to Rick. He was already on board and headed this way with the patrol boat so the perimeter of the Big Pine Key could be searched.

By the time everyone and everything had been set up and ready to go, it was pushing two o'clock. That left them with roughly five to six hours of daylight to work with. They had assembled two helicopters and a substantial ground force.

Reed and Rick would use the boats to search around the shoreline of Big Pine. The FBI wanted to concentrate efforts on the island since that is where the last two victims had been found. They were confident that he kept the girls somewhere on this island because it would be easier to dump a body than haul it around.

After their final briefing, everyone went to their designated search zones determined to find Val ... alive. Franklin approached Reed. "There's one more thing I think you should know. It's about Detective Mason's sister Brianna."

Worry gripped Reed and he asked "What about her? Valerie has been worried after receiving a strange phone call from her the other day. Don't tell me she's..."

Franklin held his hand up stopping him.

"We have her in protective custody. We have reason to believe that she was going to be the Reverend's next victim, so we took her to keep her safe."

"Valerie will be happy to know she's safe when we find her."

"We will," he said with a slap on Reed's shoulder, "We will."

~ ~ ~

Valerie had nothing to use as a weapon judging by the sheer emptiness of the room, that is if she could get out of the rope he had tied her up with. Thank God she had heard him mumbling about running out of tape. She knew that is what was used on the other two girls to bind their hands, feet, and cover their mouths. If she could get the rope off he had used on her, she could use it against him and choke him with it. Not the best or easiest of plans, but it was all she had. There was no way of knowing when he would return, so she needed to work fast. Since her hands were tied behind her back, she lay down on the mattress and moved her arms down the backs on her legs, bending them so she could slip the rope up and around so that her arms would be in front. She began working the knot with her teeth. At first it seemed she wasn't getting far, but soon she could feel it starting to loosen.

Hearing a noise outside, she paused to listen. It sounded like a helicopter flying overhead, so she continued. It took a while and her teeth and gums were sore, but it finally came undone. She quickly slid it off her wrists and loosened the ones around her ankles. She would wrap them loosely when he came back to make it look like they were still tied.

Feeling confident in the only plan she had for escape, she now had to wait for his return. She was both hopeful and scared at the same time. She was sure her friends and co-workers knew she was missing by now. Reed would have known when he returned home to find her car still at his house. He was aware that she suspected the Reverend, only he didn't know she had suspected the wrong one.

"Please let him figure it out!" she pleaded out loud. She knew they would be looking for her, but would they know where to look? She had heard a chopper not long ago. Could it be looking for her? She sighed out loud. It was probably a tourist helicopter taking visitors out for a bird's eye view of the water and islands.

Feeling tears threatening at the corners of her eyes, she took a deep breath determined not to give in to the fear. For now, all she could do was wait for Lockhart to return. Valerie paced, quoted Hemingway, and went over her escape plan again and again in her mind while waiting. She was feeling sleepy and didn't want to chance falling asleep for two reasons. The first, she might wake up and find Lockhart here trying to harm her and she wouldn't have a chance to fight back, and the second was the fact she might have a concussion and it wasn't safe to sleep right now. It was hard to fight it though because the heat inside the room was suffocating, which added to her drowsiness plus the fact she had nothing to drink.

There was very little light streaming through the only window that wasn't boarded up. It sat very close to the ceiling and was much too small to crawl through, even if she had some way of reaching it. She could tell by the length of the shadows on the wall that it was late afternoon and it wouldn't be long until the sun went down. At least it would be cooler in here then.

Walking to the door and trying to open it for the hundredth time, it still wouldn't give. There was literally nothing left for her to do but wait.

Chapter 18

Morris had his men searching the Blue Hole area and the nature trail. So far, everyone that radioed back had found no trace of Valerie. He was feeling guilty, as if somehow his friendship had blinded him to what Lockhart really was, but then again he couldn't have known. Apparently nobody had known, but that did little to appease his guilty conscious. He had to give it to the guy, his acting skills were superb.

The reverend's wife had finally been located in Miami. She had gone to stay with her sister at her husband's urging. He convinced her she needed to get away from time to time. How convenient for a serial killer to give his wife a mini vacation so he could do his dirty deeds. As for the times when Lockhart had mentioned visiting his daughter, they had learned after speaking with Mrs. Lockhart that she had died years ago. It was now believed by the FBI that her death was at her own father's hands, when he found his daughter in the backseat of her boyfriend's car, even though it could never be proven. Both kids had disappeared with the bodies being discovered eighteen months later. They were too decomposed to collect much evidence from. Animals had scattered the bones around the copse of woods they were found in, but dental records were able to identify them. The saddest part of all was that there were tiny fetus bones found close to his daughter's body, indicating she had been pregnant at the time. The cause of death remained a mystery to this day.

The reverend had told everyone that the kids had run away after being found out, and of course no one had any reason to doubt his word. Soon after they were found and buried, the Lockharts moved from Tallahassee to the Keys. He told everyone it was for his wife's sanity. After the loss of their only child, he would take her away from the memories that would haunt her daily if they stayed in Tallahassee.

She was now currently in a local hospital under a doctor's care after learning of her husband's crimes. Finding out that her husband was a serial killer was bad enough, but knowing that he might have taken their daughter's life, in addition to a potential grandchild, had proven too much for her to bear. She had suffered a heart attack and they were awaiting word from her sister as to how she was doing. He sure hoped that she pulled through.

What a damn shame. All because somewhere along the line Lockhart had gotten the idea he was the mighty sword of retribution for God, and his mission was to punish *bad* women.

Right now though, his main concern was finding Detective Mason and capturing Lockhart so he could be put away for the rest of his life. So far, no trace of her had been found. They were still scouring every square mile of the island and had not turned up any clues. There had been no sign of Lockhart either.

Reed and Rick had made it about two thirds of the way around the perimeter of the island without any luck. There were some isolated stretches of shoreline, but nothing had turned up. He was trying not to lose hope when he heard the radio crackle to life. It was the helicopter pilot. He had just spotted a black sedan off the main highway and down a small dirt road. It wasn't visible from the main highway because of a hedge of sea grape trees, which would explain why nobody had found it. The pilot said it looked like it had crashed into some palms. He radioed the coordinates to the patrol officers, but by then, Morris was already in his car and yelling for Agent Franklin to get in. He knew the exact spot the pilot was talking about. It was about two hundred yards from a bridge that he fished from with his brothers and Dad as a boy. If it was still standing, there was an old cabin under the bridge, and that could very well be where he was holding Valerie.

Franklin radioed ahead to Rick and Reed and told them to meet them at the bridge. He heard Morris blow out an exasperated breath. Poor guy. For a man that hadn't seen much more than car accidents and a few suicides over the past thirty years, he was getting all of it all at once. In less than fifteen minutes, he could be facing down a man, that for the most part, he had considered a friend and counselor for the past few years.

Arriving at the turn off, Morris said a quick prayer for everyone's safety and soon spotted the car wrapped around a trio of palm trees. He and Agent Franklin walked over to the car to find bloodstains on the seats, and hair and blood on the spider webbed windshield.

The other deputies were pulling up so Morris took a few moments to scan the surrounding area. Out of the corner of his eye, he saw movement in the tree line moving towards the bridge. He got the men's attention and motioned towards that general direction. Franklin took command and told them that they were going to spread out and surround the cabin. Morris wasn't offended in the least, he was glad someone with experience was here to help.

Reed and Rick had just arrived after anchoring close to the shoreline and using a small raft to make landfall. The anticipation was eating Reed alive and both men were filled in on the course of action they were taking. They had thought to use the element of surprise, but if Morris had seen Lockhart, he might have seen them too.

Once everyone was in position around the old run down cabin, Agent Franklin got on the speaker "Lockhart, we know you're inside and we have the cabin surrounded. Come out with your hands up."

Silence.

"Let Detective Mason walk out unharmed and we'll talk about a deal. If you harm her though, this will not end well for you."

Still no answer, but they could hear movement taking place inside. It sounded a lot like a scuffle. Morris and Reed looked at each other.

"You don't think..." Morris began.

"That Valerie would try something? Yes I do." Reed finished for him.

After several minutes with no response, Agent Franklin said, "I am tired of screwing around with his ass." He started giving orders for men to get in position to storm the cabin.

Reed was furious. "You can't go in there with guns blazing. Valerie could get hurt, or worse."

"He is not responding to us Lieutenant, she could already be hurt. We have to go in before the situation gets any worse, before he has any more time to plan an escape."

Reed knew that he was right, but couldn't shake the feeling that something really bad was about to happen, and Valerie would be on the receiving end.

~ ~ ~

Valerie heard commotion outside and figured that Lockhart had come back. She readied herself on the mattress to give the impression she was still tied up. She held the rope that had been used to tie her wrists together in her hands

He hurried through the door barely glancing her way. He didn't speak, but instead walked to the opposite corner of the room and dropped a backpack on the floor. He squatted down and unzipped it pulling out a gun. He had seen the men outside and knew that in a matter of moments they would have the cabin surrounded. He would need to use Detective Mason as a hostage. Why couldn't people see he was doing the Lord's work? The world had been brainwashed through media and movies to accept and protect the evildoers of the world instead of glorifying the innocent.

Val knew this was probably her only chance and since he seemed preoccupied. She eased off the mattress so as not to make any noise and wiggled her ankles to remove the rope she had loosely placed around them before he had come in. She used the rope from her wrists to wrap around her hands so she would have some strength when she slipped it over his head to choke him with. How ironic that he might die the same way he killed.

He turned suddenly just as she reached to put the rope around his throat startling them both. Somehow she managed to get it around his neck anyway, but only the part she needed to use to pull against his throat was now behind his neck instead of the front. He grabbed her shoulders shoving her backward but she wasn't letting go. If she was going down, he was going with her. They both crashed to the floor, nearly knocking the wind out of her when he landed on top of her. They rolled around on the floor, both struggling to get the upper hand.

"Damn it," he muttered as he finally landed on top and held her down to make her stop struggling. "Get up you idiot. You're my ticket out of here."

She could hear someone demanding he surrender and/or release her unharmed. Lockhart yanked her up by her arm with the gash on it from the car crash causing her to wince in pain. He shoved the gun into her ribcage and said, "Now move. You're gonna walk nice and slow. If you try anything else stupid, you'll be dead before you finish the thought."

He nudged her forward. She walked towards the door and opened it slowly. The two walked in tandem outside and were blinded by the strobing lights on the patrol cars. It was hard to see anything, much less make out where anyone was standing. Lockhart was pulling her towards the tree line using her as a shield.

"Let her go Lockhart."

He ignored the directive and continued towards the tree line. Valerie wondered about how good of a shot he was, and if it was worth trying to break away and run. She knew that she had to try, so when she felt ready, she ducked to the left and took off running towards the blue lights. She had only taken a few steps when she heard a popping sound, and a slow moving pain began to spread through her ribs. The last thing she remembered was hearing someone yell her name. It sounded a lot like Reed, and then blackness engulfed her.

Reed ran over to where Valerie lay crumpled in a lifeless heap on the ground.

"Call for an ambulance!"

"There's already one on the way," someone called out.

Reed snatched his shirt over his head to use it to put pressure on Val's wound and hopefully stop the bleeding. "Stay with me Val, please," He begged.

Rick ran over. "The ETA for the ambulance is about three minutes. She'll be okay man," he said trying to reassure Reed.

Those three minutes felt like a lifetime to Reed. When they finally heard the siren and saw the ambulance pull up he realized he had been holding his breath and released it. He took a big gulp of air to try to calm himself.

The EMT's had grabbed their equipment and a gurney and were working their way over to Valerie. They immediately began checking her vitals, and one of them uncovered the wound to get a better look at what they were dealing with. He checked her for an exit wound and couldn't feel one confirming that the bullet was still in her when they lifted her to put her on the gurney. They loaded her into the back of the ambulance and Reed rode with her. Not once on the way to the hospital did she open her eyes of show any signs of life, other than her faint heartbeat on the monitor. The EMT told Reed her blood pressure was low from the loss of blood, and it would be touch and go for now. It was all a waiting game.

~ ~ ~

Lockhart was close to the tree line when Valerie had broken the grip he had on her and took off running. He fired the gun, but never stopped to see if he had hit his target.

The deputies had watched everything play out as if it were in slow motion. There were multiple voices yelling, "Stop" and gunfire erupted all around him. Somehow, he managed to dodge all of their shots. This only served to reassure him that he was going to be vindicated for doing God's work and the Lord had offered his protection over him this night. He knew they were coming after him so he needed to go just a little deeper into the pines where the brush was thicker so he could squat down and hide. He would just have to wait them out. He had gone about a quarter of a mile when he heard a voice behind him.

"Lockhart!"

He turned slowly to see Detective Morris pointing a gun at him. Morris had made his way into the woods knowing that Pastor would run. Lockhart raised his own gun in defense.

"Don't try anything stupid. Put the gun down. It's over," Morris said in a voice that seemed way too calm.

"Detective, I am doing what the Lord has ordained me to do. If you think about it, you'll realize I'm right. I mean, you arrest women like these ... prostitutes and drug addicts. In no time they are back on the streets doing the same thing again and again. At least I put a stop to their sinful natures. God demands that women be virtuous. Eve started this whole thing when she committed the first sin."

"You're crazy! What about your wife? What about your daughter?"

"My wife is of noble character ... she is more precious than rubies, just as the Lord has declared in Proverbs 31:10."

"You don't have to quote scripture to me. What about your daughter? She was just a 16 year old girl."

"She was a whore! She got herself pregnant by the no good loser she was dating after I forbid her to see him. She had to be punished, and then saved."

"Do you hear yourself? You killed your daughter you sick bastard. YOUR OWN DAMN DAUGHTER!" Morris shouted. He could not contain his anger any longer.

"SHUT UP." Lockhart grabbed both sides of his head as if in tremendous pain.

"Drop the gun Lockhart."

Still holding the left side of his head, he pointed the gun at Morris. The detective, who was only a few weeks away from retirement, did the one thing he had never had to do in his entire career in law enforcement. He fired his service weapon. The bullet struck Lockhart in the left side of his chest.

"You'll ... go ... to ... hell for this," he sputtered as blood foamed from his mouth.

"You'll be there to welcome me." Morris kicked the gun away that Lockhart had dropped when he fell to the ground. He dropped to his knees beside the man who had been his friend and pastor for many years. He heard him utter one last thing "Forgive him father...he knows... not what... he does." He closed his eyes for the last time.

"Believe me father, I know exactly what I have done." Morris whispered.

When the rest of the team arrived, they found Lockhart lying on the ground dead and Morris kneeling down beside him with his head hanging down, as if in prayer.

Chapter 19

Where was that incessant beeping noise coming from? It was more annoying than the sound of an alarm clock.

Valerie struggled to open her eyes. It seemed as if they were being held shut. Had she taken a sleeping pill last night as she did from time to time to help with her insomnia?

She could feel a pressure around her chest right up under her breasts. What the…?

She finally managed to open her eyes and was disoriented. Where was she? She looked down and could see her father laid over on the edge of her bed from a chair that he was sitting in. He was holding her hand which felt numb.

She tried to speak. Her mouth was so dry but she did manage to croak out, "Daddy".

He quickly lifted his head up and smiled. "Hey baby, you're awake!" He stood up, leaning over her to kiss her forehead. "There are a lot of people who will be happy to hear you're awake." He walked over to the door to call for the nurse. The nurse's station was right across the hall from her room.

The nurse came in, and upon seeing Val awake, smiled and said "Glad to see you back among us mere mortals." She checked a couple of readings from the machines and pushed a button that ceased the beeping that had irked Valerie earlier. She crossed over to the sink and filled up a small pitcher with water and ice so Val could relieve her thirst. She carried the pitcher back over and poured a cup of water and helped Val take a few sips through a straw.

"Slowly" she told Val. She left to inform the doctor of Valerie's progress.

"Do you remember why you're here?" her dad asked.

"Vaguely. I remember Pastor Lockhart kidnapped me and then ... I was in a cabin or shed somewhere close to water I think."

Her dad sighed. She didn't remember being shot, and he had to tell her. "He tried to escape into the woods and used you as a hostage. When you tried to run from him, he shot you."

Unconsciously, she touched her bandages around her chest. "I guess that would explain these then." She said trying to use humor to ease the pain she could feel underneath those bandages. "How long have I been here?"

"Five days. They had to do surgery to remove the bullet. It nicked your lung."

"Five days?" she asked incredulously.

"You've woken up off and on briefly for the past two days but not long enough to talk or anything. Even Wonder Woman needs time to recover," Her Dad teased smiling at her.

They both remained silent for a few moments so Val could take in the magnitude of what she had endured.

"Was he caught?" she finally inquired.

"Detective Morris shot him. He's dead." Her dad never was one to mince words, and she was glad that he wasn't beating around the bush now.

"How's Detective Morris?" she asked quietly.

"He'll be fine, I'm sure. He seems like a tough old bird. Right now he is somewhere in North Carolina taking a much needed vacation. He calls every day to check on you though."

Valerie knew the detective had not seen much action like this. She would call him as soon as she was able. A shooting was always hard on any officer no matter how the media tried to portray cops. They were human beings too, and some took it really hard when they had to take a human life, even when that life was an evil one. Detective Morris had not only had to shoot a man, but one that had been his friend.

She tried to move and grimaced. Her dad told her he would go find the nurse and see about getting her some pain meds.

After her dad left she caught movement out of the corner of her eye. She looked to the side of the room that was shaded in darkness. Her heart skipped a beat when she saw Reed asleep on a couch way too small for his large frame. He stretched and almost fell off the couch, causing Val to giggle. She moaned and quickly quelled the urge to laugh. More than anything, she wanted to feel his arms around her and know that everything would be okay. He sat up rubbing his eyes and looked over at her. He moved quickly to her side when he noticed she was finally awake.

"Hey beautiful."

"Hey yourself."

"How are you feeling?"

"Like I've been shot."

He smiled and leaned over to gently brush his lips against hers.

"You gave us all a real scare you know," he said rubbing his thumb against the top of her hand.

"Yeah, sorry about that. I'll try not to do it again."

"I have some good news that will make you happy. I talked to Delaney and Rick about an hour ago to update them on your progress and they told me that they are getting married and it's all because of you."

"Me, what did I have to do with it?"

"Seeing what you've been through convinced them that life is too short to wait, and so ... Rick proposed."

"You're right. That makes me extremely happy. I can't wait to see them and congratulate them."

Her dad returned about that time with the nurse who walked over and injected some medication into the IV that would ease Val's pain.

"Is that going to make me sleepy? I think five days of sleep is quite enough."

"It's possible. It has that effect on some people, others not so much." The nurse adjusted the drip and told her if she need anything else she would be right outside. As she exited the room, Agent Franklin, AKA Pastor Cross, and Agent Giovanni entered.

"We saw your dad at the nurse's station and he told us you were awake. Glad to see you pulled through." Agent Giovanni spoke first.

Valerie looked straight at Agent Franklin and said, "I'm sorry I thought you were guilty of killing those girls Pastor."

This brought a chuckle from everyone in the room.

"What am I missing?" she asked looking around at everyone.

"Detective Mason, allow me to introduce Agent Matt Franklin. He was undercover as Pastor Anthony Cross keeping an eye on Lockhart. We've had Lockhart under investigation for a while, and needed someone who could get close to him that wouldn't arouse his suspicions, Agent Giovanni explained.

The stunned look on her face caused everyone to laugh again.

"Anything else I should know?" she asked jokingly.

Everything was explained to her in detail. Both agents had found out through their own detective work that other women staying at the shelter were at risk of being taken by Lockhart because of his association with the shelter through his church. That included Valerie's sister who was going by the name of Tammy Porter. They realized she was using an alias when they ran the women's fingerprints from the home, and her prints came back to Brianna Mason, who just happened to be Valerie's sister.

When asked about the alias, she just stated that she wanted to be anonymous at the shelter, and didn't want anyone that knew her sister contacting her and telling her where she was living. Based on surveillance of Lockhart, they thought she could be next, so they took her into protective custody and warned her not to contact anyone until this was over. Of course, true to her stubborn nature she did call her sister, but Valerie didn't understand the static filled call.

Things were beginning to make sense finally. The second victim that was found was identified as Janine Brown, who was a resident at the shelter. Through her fingerprints they discovered she had a past record that included drug use and prostitution.

Valerie sighed and leaned back on her pillow. "The woman running the shelter had asked me on Sunday to check on Janine Brown because she had not seen her in several days. Guess we know why now. What I don't understand is Ali Musgrave was not a resident there. She had a decent job and was living in her own apartment a world apart from these women."

"True. We thought the same thing. It turns out she was a generous young woman who was always taking clothing and other personal items to the shelter and volunteered some time there. Apparently, her best friend along with her mother, from high school had spent time in a shelter thanks to an abusive father, so she had a soft spot for these women. We can only guess that's how Lockhart found her, we'll never really know."

"How did you figure out where to find me?" she asked Agent Giovanni.

"That was Reed. Apparently someone told him they had seen you get in the car with a preacher."

She looked at Reed.

"It was actually Andy and Barney who saved the day."

"Excuse me, did you just say Andy and Barney?" Agent Franklin asked.

Val smiled. "Andy is a homeless guy that I give doughnuts to sometimes, and Barney is his golden retriever." Everyone had a good chuckle over that.

"Thank you guys so much for looking out for Brianna. She can be a handful sometimes."

"Don't I know it," Agent Giovanni muttered under his breath causing Val to take a good look at him.

Just as she did she heard a familiar voice. "Did I just hear my name?"

Her sister came through the door with her red curls bouncing and a big smile on her face.

Valerie was instantly reminded of the girl her sister used to be. She walked over and gave Val a big hug and with tears in her eyes she said, "I'm so glad you're ok sis."

"I'm glad *you're* ok. You look so good ... so healthy. I've heard you're taking college classes. I'm so proud of you Bri." Now Val had tears in her eyes.

"Thanks. I'm proud of myself. I've had a little help from my friends." She looked shyly at Agent Giovanni, and he winked at her. What in the world is going on there? Val wondered.

Everyone was talking amongst themselves when Al Foster appeared in the doorway with a dozen tie-dyed roses.

"Come in Mr. Foster, join the party," Val said enthusiastically.

"It's getting a bit crowded in here so Agent Franklin and I will go. We'll catch up with you in a few days to finish up all the reports." Agent Giovanni suggested. He glanced at Brianna and smiled then headed out the door.

"Ok. Thank you guys, for everything," Val said with genuine gratitude.

Mr. Foster made his way over to her side, and handed the roses to Valerie.

"These are the most beautiful and unusual roses I have ever seen in my life." She took a big whiff of them, even though their scent filled the room.

"I heard what happened and just wanted to come by to wish you well."

"Thank you so much, that means a lot to me, especially since you were considered a person of interest in the case I was working on. Not that I ever believed it for a moment."

"You were just doing your job. I understand. I'm just glad you're ok."

Reed had never left her side the entire time people had been coming and going. He suddenly said, "I have something I want to say. In light of what has taken place and what everyone has been though the last few days, especially Val, I can't think of a more appropriate time to say this." He took Val's hand and kissed it. "I love you. Even though we haven't known each other very long, I know you are the only woman I'll love for the rest of my life. I ...we almost lost you," he said looking around at everyone. "I can't describe with words how that made me feel. I don't want to think about what this world would be like without you in it. Valerie Mason, will you marry me?"

Stunned, it took her a few moments for what he said to sink in.

"Don't keep him waiting, answer the man," Her Dad instructed.

She suddenly laughed, then grabbed her ribs, and with tears in her eyes from joy and pain she said yes. Reed kissed her gently and said, "as soon as they spring you from this place, we'll go pick out a ring."

Everyone was congratulating them when Mr. Foster said, "I know a decent photographer if you need one for the wedding."

"I can't think of a better one." He gave her a gentle hug and then gave Reed a pat on the back. "I'm gonna go and leave you to rest. We'll get together soon and discuss those wedding photos."

"Thanks Mr. Foster."

"Just call me Al, please. Or tie-dye Al as most of my neighbors call me."

"Ok Al, take care. I still remember your number, 555-2782, so I'll give you a call." He smiled a bright smile and shaking his head, walked out with a little wave.

The nurse came barreling in like a bull in full charge and told everyone they would have to leave, with the exception of one family member. Valerie needed some rest the nurse insisted, which Val thought was ridiculous given she had slept for five days, but she was feeling a bit tired.

Everyone was getting prepared to leave and Valerie looked at Reed. "Would you mind if my dad stayed? I kind of need my daddy right now."

"No sweetheart, I understand. We have the rest of our lives together. You haven't seen him in a while. Besides, I need to go tell my parents the good news. They send their well wishes by the way."

"Thanks. I love you." She said realizing it was the first time she had said it and how good it felt.

"Love you too." He leaned over and kissed her forehead.

"Are you sure you want your old man to stay, and not your future husband?' her dad asked.

"Yes, I'm sure. We have a lot of catching up to do."

"I told you. I'm not going anywhere. I need to be with my girls. All of this has helped me see that. Sorry I haven't been here all along." He looked deflated.

"No regrets dad. It is what it is. But since I'm getting married, and you're moving, I know a great houseboat you can buy." They both started chuckling.

"I guess it all works out then," he said. "Try and rest. I'll be right here when you wake up."

Val closed her eyes and her heart was full. She was engaged to the man of her dreams, her best friend was also getting married, her dad was moving to be closer to his girls and her sister was on the right path ... finally.

Val felt blessed just to be alive.

Epilogue
One Year Later

Guests were steadily pouring into the gardens of the Hemingway Home where a wedding would take place in a little under an hour.

Reed was filling the role of the nervous groom, while his parents were busy directing waiters on where to put the trays of hors d'oeuvres that had come from the Bistro. He was anxious to see his beautiful bride walk down the aisle. The past year had been full of recovery for Valerie, and getting to know each other. His proposal had been a fast one, and they had decided it was best to wait a while before tying the knot. He was sure he wanted to be with her the rest of his life, but he gave her the space she needed after everything she had been through.

Rick and Delaney had also been married six months ago and Valerie didn't want it to seem as if she and Reed were trying to show them up, so there was yet another reason for them to wait. Rick was talking with a guest and Delaney, of course, was with Val getting ready to walk down the aisle as a bridesmaid.

Al Foster had been out here taking pictures of guests, but was now in the waiting room with the bride and her party taking some shots of them.

He scanned the crowd and could see that Detective Morris and his wife had just arrived and were being ushered to their seats, as well a few other deputies they both worked with. Agent Giovanni was there as Brianna's "plus one." He and Val were sure there was something going on between them, but every time they asked Brianna insisted they were only friends. Time would tell he guessed.

Valerie had invited Andy and Barney, since they had set Reed on the right trail to finding her. They had bought him a nice pair of dress clothes and paid for him to have a shave and haircut. They had also taken the dog to be groomed. He was sporting a bow tie around the neck.

He felt a tap on the shoulder and turned around to find his brother Jason standing there in his tux, ready to be a groomsman.

"Well little brother, guess your freedom is about to be over. No more girlfriend of the month club for you!" he teased with a huge grin.

"I'm good with that. Valerie is more than enough to keep me happy."

"Then I'm happy for you."

Just then their mother walked over and put her hands of each of their cheeks.

"My handsome boys."

They were both a little embarrassed but indulged her. She rarely had her family all together anymore, so she was excited.

The new pastor of the Church of the Islands, the church that had been subject to so much scrutiny in the press after Lockhart had been found out, indicated that the ceremony was about to begin and that everyone needed to take their places. Al Foster came out of the little room where Val was waiting and took position to get her coming down the aisle. His girlfriend, Beverly Gail also had a camera so she could get the look on Reed's face as he saw his bride for the first time in her gown.

A hush fell over the crowd gathered and soft music began to play. There were only two attendants, Delaney and Brianna. Val considered both of them

Matron and Maid of honor. The same for Reed, his brother and Rick were both Best Men.

Delaney and Brianna came walking out slowly in strapless knee length sundresses that were a soft yellow. They both carried bouquets that were a mixture of orange and yellow orchids, and seashells.

Valerie stepped out of the doorway with her father. Everyone stood as the bridal march began to play. He looked every bit the proud papa.

Her tea-length white dress was so simple yet, elegant. She looked radiant as the sun was beginning to set, giving everything an ethereal feel and glow. She wore her hair in an upsweep with a few tendrils handing down and a crown of baby's breath entwined in it.

She took Reed's breath away. He didn't think she could be any more beautiful than she already was, but here she was proving him wrong. She walked up to him and her father placed her hand in Reed's. The rest of the next few moments were a blur, then they were pronounced husband and wife.

They looked into each other's eyes and kissed gently as their friends and families cheered them on. Without having to speak a word, they both knew, this was the first of many happy occasions for them, because living in paradise, even the worst days wouldn't seem so bad.

About the Author

After health issues caused Angela Jarvis to quit her job as a Physical Therapy Technician, she decided to devote more time to writing, which she has loved since her early teens. Angela lives in a very small town on the southern edge of Lake Okeechobee with her husband, daughter, and several fur babies. She has a grown son who is a sheriff deputy in the Florida Panhandle. He is a good source of information about law enforcement. "I find that ideas abound in a small town," says Angela. "Watching and listening is where all my best ideas come from."

Acknowledgements

I am thankful to my parents for telling me I could be anything or anyone as long as I worked hard, and especially mom for passing on her love of reading to me. To my husband and kids, I love you more than life and thank you for believing in me.

To my high school English teacher Sylvia Plumey, thank you for believing in my writing enough that you use my old high school work to teach others.

And last but not least

The inspiration for Al Foster---Mickey AKA the Hippie Paparazzi. Your love, kindness and generosity knows no bounds. Thank you for a place to stay while I was researching Big Pine.

ABSOLUTELY AMAZING eBOOKS

AbsolutelyAmazingEbooks.com

or AA-eBooks.com

www.ingramcontent.com/pod-product-compliance
Lightning Source LLC
Chambersburg PA
CBHW050358030726
47503CB00006B/1917